TOOL

RUTHLESS KINGS BOOK 3

K.L. Savage

ISBN: 978-1-952500-03-9
LIBRARY OF CONGRESS CONTROL: 2020907900

PHOTOGRAPHY BY WANDER AGUIAR PHOTOGRAPHY
COVER MODEL: CHRIS FLEMING AND JAKE

COVER DESIGN: KARI MARCH DESIGNS
Editing and Formatting: MASQUE OF THE RED PEN
FIRST EDITION PRINT 2020

DEDICATION

To anyone who thought they were a burden to love, love has no burdens, no fears, it accepts you for who you are, damaged, afraid, and wild. The only burden is doubt. You're deserving of love. Doubt has no home here.

Fifteen years old

Love is a supernatural entity that has never lived here; not on this planet, not in this town, and definitely not in this home. Hell, to call this house a home is a lie. It's nothing but a prison, keeping us locked up like stray animals. If love does exist, it doesn't find me or my mom worthy of it.

That's fine.

Fuck love. Fuck what it brings.

From what I've noticed, love only brings control and pain.

Hate is born from love, and it's all I've ever felt because of him.

My dad.

My drunk of a father who only works part-time because he can't find a job that will keep his drunk ass. My mom is the star, the heavy lifter, the one who kills herself every day to make sure there is food on the table, that the electricity stays on, so we have a warm bed to sleep in at night, and a roof over our head.

She also is the reason why his ass never leaves the recliner. I swear to god his body has molded to the old green chair. It smells of him, beer and body odor. He goes days without showering, and all of his clothes are filthy with stains. It isn't because my mom doesn't wash them; she does. He's just that disgusting.

I'm waiting for the day I turn eighteen so I can get my mom out of here. I can't do anything for her yet. I'm just skin and bone and a kid. I can't do shit to stop him, and nothing pisses me off more. I hate him with every cell in my body.

I hate that I come from him.

I hate that I look like him.

I've done all that I can to work out, to put meat on my bones, to learn how to fight, but I don't eat enough for the muscle to stick. My dad won't allow it. He eats all he wants first, then Mom and I can have the scraps.

He thinks he's a king.

And I can't wait to rip him from his throne—that fucking nasty chair that smells of mistakes and cigarettes.

"See you at school tomorrow, Logan!" my friend Kent shouts as we get off the bus.

Snow crunches under my boots as I walk to the rundown duplex I live in. It's old, the paint is chipping, windows are cracked, and the mailbox leans. I told my mom that when the snow melts,

I'll work on the house and clean it up. Mom is ashamed of where we live and I don't want her to be. She deserves more than this cold hell we find ourselves living in.

Literally, it's fucking cold. I hate Boston. There is a foot of snow on the ground, and it just keeps coming, thick fluffy flakes landing on my face and coat. I'm sick of it.

"See you, Kent," I say, waving as I cross the frozen street. It's white from salt, ice, and snow. A bit slick, and if someone isn't careful, they can slip and bust their ass. I have more than once, and it sucks. Last time it happened, I couldn't sit down for three weeks without crying out in complete agony.

Which then got me a slap across the face from my dad. He said, "Boys don't fucking cry. No boy of mine will tear up like a little bitch. Is that what you are? A bitch? Like your mom?"

My mom stood behind him with a black eye, and I saw the look in her eyes; the pleading desperation for me to keep my mouth shut, so I did what she wanted.

I rub my cheek from the memory, and I can almost feel the burn of his hand and the tingle underneath my skin as his palm made impact. Stopping at the gate, I reach around the broken tips of what used to be a white picket fence and unlatch the iron lock and push it open, only for it to fall off its hinges and onto the ground. "You've got to be kidding me," I mumble, shoving my backpack up my shoulder as I reach down to pick up the rotted wood. I spin around and lean the entrance of the gate against the fence and walk down the cracked cement walkway that's covered in bits of salt I put out this morning. I stomp my feet as I climb up the stairs to get the snow off.

If I track any inside, I'll get a belt to my back for fifteen minutes. My shoulder is still tender from the beating I got yesterday. I look down to make sure the snow is off my boots, and it is, but I don't want to chance it. I slide them off my feet and leave them by the door. My feet are frozen since the socks I have has holes in them.

I hate being broke. I hate that my mom works her ass off, and he takes her hard-earned money. I want to drop out of high school and get a job, then me and my mom can get out of here, but she says no, that education is important, and she'll deal with my father until we can figure out something else.

The screen door creaks as I open it, then push the main door open with my hip. Damn it, he's home. I can smell the fresh lit cigarette lingering in the hallway. He tracked snow in! I can still see his boot prints. The fucking irony of him.

Loud banging comes from the kitchen followed by my mom's too familiar painful yell. I drop my bag and run down the hall to see my dad pinning her against the table. "You stupid bitch!" he slurs, wrapping his hand around her throat. "I said get me a fucking beer, and you're going to get me that damn beer!" he roars, and she flinches away. The light shines on her cheeks illuminating her tears and busted lip.

"We don't have any money, Fred. I got us groceries. We didn't have enough for beer."

He slaps her again, and her head snaps to the left. She holds one of her delicate hands to her face, the same hands that make sure I live to see another day, and her eyes meet mine. She must see the rage on my face, but she shakes her head again, telling me to stay back.

Mom is always looking out for me, but when am I going to start looking out for her? She deserves more from me.

"Look at me, whore," he sneers at her, leaning his body onto hers. I know she's uncomfortable. He's a fat fuck with a beer belly. "You're cheating on me, aren't you? You spreading your legs for someone else? Who would want you? You're an ugly, stupid cunt who doesn't know her place." He takes her by the throat and throws her onto the kitchen floor. "Maybe I need to remind you who you belong to, woman." He reaches for the button on his pants, and my mother turns on her belly, trying to crawl a way.

Oh, fuck no. He isn't going to touch her. He isn't going to get near her, ever again. This shit stops now. My mom will no longer be a victim to his mental, physical, or emotional abuse. She will no longer be raped or beaten by him.

He drops his pants and falls to the floor on his knees and grabs her ankles. She kicks and screams, pleading no, and I push off the wall and slam into him, knocking him on the ground. "You sonofabitch!" I scream in his face. "You won't touch her! You understand?" I bring my fist up and let it fly, slamming my knuckles against his face. "I hate you! You're the worthless one, you useless"—punch—"fucking"—punch—"drunk!" Punch.

9

He grabs me by my shirt and throws me off him, and my head hits the cabinets.

"Logan!" My mother reaches for me, but he grabs her legs, and I push myself up onto my feet and tackle him again. We fly across the kitchen table, and I fist his shirt, pick him up, and then slam him on the floor.

I'm going to kill him.

"That all you got, boy?" He laughs, his yellow rotted teeth are covered with blood. I did that. I hurt him. I made the fucker bleed.

And I'm happy about it.

"You don't have the balls to do anything to me."

"Logan." My mother's voice is pleading, but I can tell she has no idea what she wants me to do. Her voice distracts me, and my dad takes that moment to get the upper hand and roll me onto my back. This time, it's his fist that lands on my cheek.

Twice, three times, and I feel the bone break.

"I never wanted you," he says through a chuckle, hovering over my face, and I have no choice but to inhale the stench of beer and nicotine. "Your mom got pregnant, and suddenly I was stuck with both of you. You're a waste of goddamn space!" His blood-ridden spit hits me in the face as he speaks. "I should have made your mother abort you, but she wanted you. I don't know why. You're pathetic." He punches me again. "And no son of mine!" Through the swollen eyelid, I see his clenched fist preparing to hit me. He'll kill me this time.

10

"You get away from my son!" my mother screams and swings an iron skillet at him, but she misses, and it hits his back instead of his head. She's so small, so tiny, all bone. She couldn't hold the skillet up long enough to hit him where she wanted to, but that's okay. It knocks the air out of my dad's lungs, and it's all I need to kick him off me and flip him to his back again.

"I'm going to kill the both of you," he says. "And finally, I'll be free." He reaches for something beside him, and when I see what it is, I act quicker than he can.

It's a screwdriver.

"No!" I wrap my fingers around the blue handle. "It's us who will finally be free of you." My heart pounds, adrenaline and rage pump through my veins, and it's unlike anything I've ever felt. I'm high on it. I bring the screwdriver in the air and slam it down right between his eyes, the same eyes that I have. The metal pierces his skull and hits his brain until it's lodged against the blue handle.

I fall backward, gasping for air, sweating. I wait for the panic to hit, but I don't feel it.

"Oh my god, Logan!" My mom wraps her arms around me and drags me off my dead father. His eyes are open as he looks up at the ceiling. "Are you okay? Baby, talk to me." Mom cries as she touches my swollen cheek.

"I couldn't let him hurt you anymore, Mom." I finally bring my eyes from my dad to her face. It's been so long that I've seen her without a bruise, I've forgotten what she looks like. "I couldn't."

"I know." She nods and kisses my forehead. "I know, baby.

It's okay. We will figure it out. We need to pack, okay? I know people who can help with this. Go pack. Let me take care of this. I love you, Logan."

"I love you too, Mom." I feel the emotion welling up in my eyes. We haven't been able to say that to each other in years because of Dad. He'd beat us then say that love doesn't live here.

It didn't. Evil will forever live in this house, and the sooner I get out of it, the better, before it turns my sanity into madness like it did my dad.

She helps us off the ground, and my eyes wander back to Dad. Blood flows from the back of his head, pooling around him. She reaches for the phone with shaky hands, and I stand there, my feet frozen to the ground as I stare at him.

He's actually dead.

I can breathe again.

"Knox, is Brass there?" my mom asks. Who the hell is Knox? What kind of name is Brass? "I'm calling in that favor. I need to get out of Boston, Brass. He's dead. Thank you. Thank you." She hangs up the phone, and I turn to her, curious.

"Who was that?" My hands are shaking, and my entire body is trembling. Has it become colder? My teeth chatter as if winter has made itself welcome inside.

"The men who are going to get us out of here and make sure your dad's body is dealt with. Go pack a bag." She pushes me, and it makes me find my feet. I nod and run to my bedroom. I pack everything I can, all the clothes that will fit in the suitcase along with a few pictures of me and my mom.

When I hurry out of the bedroom, I hear a grumble of motorcycles pull up, and a stampede of boots fill the hallway. "Whitney? Whitney!" a deep voice booms through the thin walls of the house, shaking them.

"In here," my mom answers him in a voice that's uneven and pitchy.

When I get to the living room, I dump the duffle bag and see four men standing around. They are huge, black jeans, big boots, leather vests that have a skull and crown. It says 'Ruthless Kings' Boston chapter. They are intimidating. I've never seen men so big in my life. I run over to my mom and push her behind me, tilting my neck as far back as I can to stare a man I don't know in the face.

He has long brown hair over his shoulders, a goatee, young-ish looking, and there's a patch on the front of his vest that says 'Brass, MC President.'

What the hell is an MC?

"You got some stones, skinny," he says, staring down at me and then my dad's dead body.

"I won't let you hurt my mom," I tell him, ignoring the fact that he called me skinny. He's a foot taller than me and has one-hundred and fifty pounds more than I do to beat me with, but I'll take him, just like I took on my father.

"They're here to help, Logan. They're friends," my mom says to me, rubbing my shoulders to help me relax.

What kind of friends does my mom make?

"You do this, kid?" Brass asks me, pointing to the body on the floor.

I swallow and nod.

"You got some fucking stones," he repeats. "You'll do just fine in life. Whitney, here. Take this. Map and money. You'll be safe in Vegas. The Ruthless chapter will help you there."

"Thank you, Brass. Thank you."

"Anything for you, Whitney," he tells her, but with a soft tone to his voice. "Prospect? Get the lye; we got work to do," he barks at a man who's green in the face and about to be sick.

"Yes, Prez." The prospect hurries away like the devil is biting at his heels.

"Knox, get them a car, then get them to the halfway point," Brass tells a guy that has VP on his vest.

They usher us out of the house, and I push between them to run back to my dad. "Wait!" They pause in picking up my dad's fat body, and I squat down, wrap my hands around the tool, and yank it free. His skull gives a sick crunch, and his brains are wet, almost making me gag, but I keep my puke down. I don't want to seem like a bitch in front of these bikers.

"Wicked," one of the bikers says.

"Taking a souvenir, skinny?" Brass asks me.

I nod, go to the sink, and clean it off, then stuff the screwdriver in my back pocket. Hell yeah, I'm taking it with me.

To remind me of the place I come from, the things I've seen, and what I'm capable of doing.

Present

"Right there. Yeah, that's it. That's the fucking spot, Becks," I praise her as she rubs my shoulders to get a knot out that's been killing me for the last few weeks. Everyone thought Becks came here to be a cut-slut, but come to find out, she didn't fuck; she just gave massages. We call her a hang-around instead. Reaper designated her as the club massage therapist, and she gets paid well for it.

Her little hands are packed with a punch. It's amazing that she can get her palms over the swell of my trap muscles, but she does and does it well.

"Oh, yeah, you're all wound up, Tool."

"Working on cars all day does that."

All too soon, the buzzer goes off telling me it's been the best sixty minutes of my life. "No," I whine. I actually whine because I'm not ready for my massage to end. "I'll pay for another hour."

"Sorry, Tool. I have back to back massages today. You bikers keep me busy." She'd really be busy if she opened her legs for the members, but she isn't that kind of woman, and I respect that. I don't even dip my dick in the cut-sluts these days. After Reaper found Sarah, and Boomer is off in Atlantic City being in love and shit, the hit it and quit it life got kind of old.

Not that I'm taking any notes from Boomer. I'm still mad at him for ditching us, but things aren't as strained as they used to be all those months ago.

"Fine," I pout and hand her a hundred-dollar bill. She racks up here. I swear, I'm in the wrong damn business. "Think I could be a massage therapist?" I ask her, thinking I really should change my ways.

She snorts and stuffs the money in her pocket. "Hell no. You aren't cute enough."

"Hey! I'm cute!" I defend myself and instantly cover my nipples with my palms, feeling a bit vulnerable and used. It's all in good fun, especially when Becks throws her head back and laughs.

See? Fun.

"If you call a shark cute," she mumbles.

I gasp, putting my hand to my chest. "Now that's crossing the line, Becks." She's right. I'll scare off clientele being six-foot-three and two-hundred and forty pounds of solid muscle. I'm tattooed pretty much all over my body. Getting ink makes me relax, so I've had a lot of stressed out times in my life considering the only place I have blank is my left ring finger.

Even if I have a jaded aspect of love, part of me thinks I'll find it one day. It's dumb.

"Bye, Tool," she sings, waving as she leaves my room to go on to her next client.

I fall back on the bed and sink into the mattress. I could fall asleep right now I'm so relaxed, but Reaper wants me to go see him, and no one ever denies the President what he wants. With a groan, I roll out of bed and rub my hands over my face. It's time to get the day started. I make my way toward the dresser and grab a soft black T-shirt that's been washed one too many times, causing it to be the most comfortable damn thing I own.

Next, I slide on a pair of grease-stained jeans and my cut, followed by my boots. A loud whoop comes from the main room, and I sigh. I never thought I'd ever come to this decision, but I want my own place. I'm tired of living here. Tired of the loud music and constant partying. Like Reaper, I'm ready to be out on my own. Reaper and Sarah moved out of the clubhouse last week and built a house on the property.

It's something I want to talk to him about. I also want to bring up an idea I've been considering for a while, since the Prez is trying to get us on the more legal side of things. I'm not sure how the meeting will go since I also manage Kings' Garage. It's also on the property. It's kind of like we have our own town on the outskirts of Vegas. Our property is gated, safe and secure, and it's getting larger by the day, but I want us to branch out more.

I want the Ruthless Kings on the Vegas strip.

I come out of my room and shut the door to find Poodle leaning against the bar talking to Skirt. Poodle has his damn sissy ass dog with him, and I always give him shit for it. While I walk, I tuck my handy dandy screwdriver behind my ear and make my way up to the two idiots.

"She won first place, Skirt. You should have seen her. She did perfect. Look at this big blue ribbon! She's so damn pretty; isn't that right, Lady? Who's a good girl? Who's the best girl?" He makes his voice all high-pitched as if he's talking to a baby and then makes kissy noises at her.

She returns his affection with a kiss of her own, licking him on the cheek. For a sissy dog, she is adorable. She's a standard poodle with groomed fluffy white hair and has one bow placed on both ears. Poodle lavishes that dog with anything and everything. He even takes her to this doggy spa, for her to relax after one of her shows.

Are you fucking kidding me? A spa for dogs to relax.

"Aye, I bet she looked like a white fluffy cloud trottin' about. Ain't that right, Lady?" Skirt scratches under Lady's chin, and she leans into it, adoring the attention.

Poodle sees me and his eyes harden as he stands up straighter, stepping in front of Lady to protect her. I would never hurt an animal, they're too damn cute, but a human?

I'll hurt a human and won't even blink doing it.

"Tool."

"Poodle," I greet, trying to peek around his body to get a look at the little prissy dog he loves so much. "Heard your Lady won a beauty contest." His face goes from white to red with anger. I love calling them beauty contests. Poodle is so damn serious about these dog shows that I can't help but give him shit for it. I mean, he runs around in a circle, with his cut on in biker boots, with a dog that makes more money than he does. Lady is the kind of dog a governor or a lawyer would have, not a biker.

"They are AKC registered dog shows, Tool! And if you knew how hard Lady trained—"

"Oh, give me a break." I roll my eyes as he tries to tell me how much Lady has put into this show business. As if it's actually blood, sweat, and tears.

Well, maybe for Poodle because … he's a bitch.

I love 'em for it, though.

"You know, I've been thinking about getting a dog," I tell him and watch as his facial expression changes.

Poodle gasps, looking offended. "Why on earth would you do that to a dog?"

Skirt tosses his head back and laughs; it's hearty and loud. It's the kind of laugh people can't help but smile at. He almost laughs like Santa Clause. Oh, now there's an idea. I'll have to bring it up with Reaper about Skirt being Santa at the children's hospital this year. I refuse to do it. The outfit makes my balls itch.

"Tool!" Reaper's voice bellows from down the hall, and I

curse. How can I forget about a meeting I just reminded myself about?

"This conversation isn't over," I tell Poodle. "I'll see you around, Lady."

"You'll do no such thing! You'll stay away from my award-winning dog, Tool."

I let out an evil chuckle as I walk down the hall to the kitchen. Once I'm out of Poodle's sight, I put on my game face for Prez, but first, I need coffee. I stop in front of the huge coffee pot—the kind found in restaurants—and grab the one without the orange handle.

"Orange means decaf. Orange means decaf," I chant to remind myself what Sarah told me a few weeks ago. We only have decaf because Reaper wants to make sure he has it on hand for when Sarah gets pregnant. We don't ever talk about babies with her. It's a touchy subject. Everyone knows a few months ago she had a miscarriage, and now she and Reaper have been trying ever since. It will happen, that I believe, but it isn't easy for her at all.

I pour myself a mug of the black java and inhale the rich goodness.

"Hi."

I jump, spill the burning hot coffee all over my hands when I see Tongue standing in the doorway, picking his nails with his blade. "Fucking hell, Tongue. You have to stop creeping up on people." I put the mug down on the counter and get a paper towel to clean myself up.

"I've been here the entire time," he drawls slowly and leans against the wall, a boot propped up on the trim.

"You have not. No one was in here when I came in."

"Maybe you should be more aware of your surroundings, Tool. Wouldn't want anyone to get the upper hand on you," he says all too casually.

"Don't you have blades to sharpen or something? I need to meet with Reaper." I pour another cup of coffee since I'm wearing the first cup and walk out of the kitchen and down another hall. The wall is lined with pictures from the previous generation of Ruthless Kings, from worn black and white photos to recent colored ones; it shows history. Reaper's dad was the President when my mom and I arrived all those years ago, and that man saved our life.

I owe everything to this club. No matter how much time has gone by, I'll never be able to fully repay what the Ruthless Kings have done for me.

The last picture is all of us on Sarah's prom night. "Damn, I fucking look good in a suit," I say out loud when my eyes land on myself. "I clean up good. I don't give a fuck what Poodle says." That little shit. He's becoming the bane of my existence. He's like the little brother I never always wanted.

Yes, never always because sometimes I do and other times I don't.

"They say talking to yourself is a form of insanity." Reaper's low voice makes me stand up a bit straighter. He's my best friend, but he's still in charge, and he deserves respect.

"Have you met Tongue?" I retort, snorting before taking a sip of my coffee.

A sudden brush of something breezes by my hair and pierces wall in front of me. "I heard that." Tongue's voice slithers like a snake in the dark hallway from ... somewhere that it isn't anywhere near me.

I glance down to the floor to see a piece of my black hair by my boot. My heart pounds. No. Not the hair. Not my fucking hair. I tilt my head up to see his knife sticking out of the wall then back down at my hair.

"Remember, I don't miss, I got what I wanted." Tongue cackles with what sounds like hysteria.

"He cut my hair!" My voice cracks. "Shit, Reaper. Does it look bad? No, don't tell me. I can't take it." I pat the side and see if I can feel the missing piece. I hope it isn't noticeable.

Reaper grabs me by the cut and throws me into his office. I'm barely able to keep the coffee from spilling again as the door slams. "Grow a pair. It's hair. Not the end of the world. It will grow back."

I stick out my bottom lip and sit in the leather chair. "It might not."

He gives me a look that dares me to say something else, but I keep my mouth shut. I bring the mug to my lips and slurp the coffee down my throat as Reaper leans back in his chair, puts his boots up on the table, and laces his fingers behind his head. "You wanted to talk? I have fifteen minutes before Sarah and I need to leave for the specialist."

"How's she doing?" I ask quietly, worried for Sarah. She's a little sister to most of us, and knowing how much she's hurting sucks because we can't do anything about it.

"She's good."

I'll have to ask Tongue what's really going on. He and Sarah are thick as thieves somehow. "How's Moretti?" He's been in a coma since the hotel explosion, and for his protection, he's been recovering in the basement. I haven't been down there in a few days to check on him, but it's hard to see him like that; laying there with burns all over his body.

"No change. Doc says he has great brain activity. He doesn't know why Moretti won't wake up."

"He will when he's ready," I say, confident that Moretti, our new friend, will wake up ready to take on the mob world again. I know his men aren't liking it here. It's "too dirty" for their liking.

So they say.

"You gonna to get to the point, Tool? Or do you want to ask about everyone in the club? You're the VP; you should know these things."

I lift my brows, a bit shocked with the annoyance and clipped tone in his voice.

He blows out a breath, puffing out his cheeks. "Fuck, I'm sorry, Tool. It's been a long few months." He runs a hand down his face, and that's when I notice just how tired he is. He looks like he has aged ten years with more silver decorating his hair and beard.

"You okay?"

"Yeah, thanks for asking. Just worn out. What can I help you with?" He changes the subject from himself to the matters at hand. Typical Reaper. He doesn't like to talk about himself.

"Well, I was wondering if I could build my own place on the property? I'm tired of clubhouse living."

"Hell yeah, you know it. Skirt is great at construction. He built our house. I'll tell him to meet with you."

"Does he work in a kilt too? Knowing I can see a big, white ass with red hair at any time makes me a little sick."

Reaper chuckles. "He does. You'll see ass too. My house is solid, though, so if the man wants to wear his kilt, I don't care. I want quality work."

"Fine," I grumble. I'll need to make sure I never put myself in the position to see his ass.

"That it?" Reaper slams his heavy boots on the floor and takes his pen in hand, getting ready to cross our meeting off his calendar.

I scratch the side of my shaved scalp and hum. "Ah, um, no. I …want to open up a business on the strip. I think it will be good for the club to get back out there. Like a live music type bar, no shady shit. Just good music and booze. I'm thinking it can be called 'Kings Club'." I stretch my hand through the air to make it look like I'm painting a vivid picture. He doesn't say anything, so I continue. "I have the money to buy the place already, but since it will be club owned, whatever revenue comes in will be the club's.

It's a good way to make legal money, Reap." He remains quiet, so I continue. "I know we have the garage and a few other things, but it's Vegas. We would—"

He holds up a hand to stop me from saying any more, and I take a big swallow of hot coffee, scalding the back of my throat. My pulse jumps on the side of my neck as I wait for the Prez to answer me.

"It sounds like a fucking fantastic idea. Are you going to have a kitchen in the club?"

"Just bar food," I tell him, and he doesn't look impressed by the frown that immediately takes over his mouth.

"I think bar food for lunch is good, but for dinner, we should keep it a little classy; show Vegas we aren't all that bad, you know?"

I nod, letting his words roll around in my head a bit. "Yeah, that can work. I just need to pick out the space."

"Take Bullseye with you to look. He's healed enough now to go out, plus he's getting grumpy. He's been threatening to kill everyone with a dart," Reaper snickers, but I don't doubt Bullseye. That guy is too talented when it comes to darts, and I'm not going to be the guy to piss him off.

"Good idea. This project will keep him busy, get him out of the clubhouse. He can't ride yet, right?"

"No, not yet. You should..." Reaper can't even get the words out because he starts laughing so hard. "You should get one of those little carts that you attach to your bike." His laugh gets all

27

pitchy, and his eyes start to water. "Can you imagine that big fucker in that side cart?"

Both of us are hollering now, slapping our knees at the thought of Bullseye sitting there with a helmet and big goggles.

"Alright, alright. I need to get going. Ah, I needed that." He takes a few deep breaths, and I stand, getting ready to go. "Keep me updated, alright? I'm excited for you, Tool. You deserve this."

I tilt my mouth in a half smile and knock my knuckles on the trim as I make my way out and down the hallway. I take a right when I get to the kitchen and go down the hall to enter the main room when I'm blinded by Skirt's ass.

He's bent over, petting Lady, and his ass and balls are on display for the entire world to see. "My eyes! Oh god! Bleach, somebody!" I cover my eyes and stumble as I walk to figure out my way without looking.

"Ye just jealous yer balls aren't as big as mine, Tool."

I'll never be able to make sure I don't see his ass. Skirt is too unexpected. One minute it's deep laughs, the next we get flashed with ginger roots. "You've stolen my soul," I say painfully, clutching my chest.

"What soul?" Poodle mutters.

"How do ye think I get all this sexy hair, lad? I've gained plenty of souls," he tells me as-a-matter-of-factly with a cheeky grin.

He might be a hairy fucker, but he's trusted, and that's all that matters to me.

"Dad, you have to let me go." I place my hands on my hips and glare at him. I understand I'm his only daughter, his only child, but I can't live in the same house as my dad for the rest of my life. I'm twenty-five-years-old. It's time for me to spread my wings, or whatever the hell women do who are my age.

"Pumpkin, I don't want you to go. You're safe here. Don't you like it?"

"Oh no!" I shake my finger at him when I see him giving me the sad dad eyes. They're real, and they affect me way too much. It's how he got me to stay here all through college. And I'm not going to fall for it anymore. "You don't get to pull that on me. I've done everything you've asked, and I want my own life. I love you, you know that, but it's time for me to move out, Dad. You know it. Plus, it isn't like you aren't going to have my apartment patrolled every second of every day," I accuse him with a small smile.

"I don't know what you're talking about," he grumbles under a breath, adjusting the belt that carries his gun, cuffs, and a few other things that I don't want to know about. My father is the sheriff of Las Vegas. There are things he does that are dangerous and life-threatening, and the less I know the better.

It sounds naïve, and maybe I want it that way. I like being blissfully unaware when it comes to his job unless I absolutely have to be. I worry about him every single day. The worry never goes away. It never fades. Every time he puts on that uniform and walks out the door, I wonder if it will be the last time I'll see him.

My dad is my best friend and without him… I rub the ache that starts to form in my chest; I don't even want to think about it. It hurts too much. I've been hoping he will retire in the next few years and relax, and then maybe I'll stop worrying all the time.

"Dad." I take two strides until I'm standing in front of him, placing my hands on his shoulders. "I know you're going to worry, but I want to make my own life. I love you. This has nothing to do with you." It does. I'm twenty-five and a virgin. Not because I want to be, but because boys aren't allowed in the house. Somehow, every time I go out on a date with a man, right when it gets hot and heavy, one of my dad's deputies knocks on the window of the car and ruins it.

I need to be out on my own because my dad is the biggest cockblock there is. I want to grow up. I want to feel like a real woman, and having my virginity doesn't make me feel like that.

"I'll be okay," I tell him, and his blue eyes shine with tears.

He knows I'm right; he just isn't happy about it. "You taught me all those self-defense moves, remember? I have the gun in my purse, and I know to keep one under my mattress with the safety on."

"But what if it isn't enough, pumpkin? I'll die if I'm not there to protect you."

"I'll be okay. The chances of anything happening are slim to none. I'm the sheriff's daughter. Men don't even ask me on a date anymore."

"Good. You can't date until you're thirty, remember?"

Oh, man. No way am I going to listen to that rule. I want to be married by the time I'm thirty. "Right. Sure, Dad." I pat his shoulder, and he sighs. I know that sound. It's the sound that says, 'Fine, I give up. Have it your way.'

"Do you have everything already packed in the truck?"

"The only thing that needs to go is me."

"Alright. Won't you need help? Let me call some of my guys—"

"Dad, I want to do this alone. Anything that I can't manage, I'll let you know; okay?"

"So independent." He brushes a piece of my dark brown hair out of my face. "Just like your mom. You look just like her, you know," he tells me, his eyes darting around my face. "Same dark hair, same green eyes, same beauty on your cheek. It's remarkable."

He tells me I look like my mom every chance he can. It's been ten years now, and I don't think he'll ever move on. He misses her. "So pretty," he says, and his blue eyes close for a second as he gathers himself. He opens his eyes and smiles, the calm and collected Sheriff Derek Johnson.

"Okay, pumpkin. Call me if you need me, okay? Seriously, I put myself as one in your speed dial. My office is two and 911 is three."

"Dad, why wouldn't I just call 911 first? You're doing your panicky thing."

"Right, you're right. Okay, dinner at your new place this weekend?"

I throw my arms around his neck, and his scruffy gray beard scratches my cheek. "You bet. I love you. I need to go. The agent is there waiting to give me the key."

"Alright, go on."

"I'll only be a few blocks away. Remember? You act like I'm leaving the state," I remind him with a roll of my eyes as I give him one last hug and then walk away. My new Honda Civic is being pulled behind the U-Haul, so I get to drive the monstrous truck. With my cute silver studded blue purse in hand, I hike it up my shoulder and take the truck key off the coffee table near the door. "I'll call you tonight. Love you."

"Love you too, Juliette. Be careful. Don't talk to strangers."

"Good lord," I mumble, walking out the door. I love him, but he is overprotective and overbearing. I've told him so many times to treat me like an adult, but as long as I live with him, that is never going to happen. That's why I'm climbing in the U-Haul on this beautiful hot day in Vegas.

I slide the key in the ignition and crank it. It growls at me for a second before the engine finally purrs to life. My dad waves as he stands by the window, and something crosses his eyes; something I have never seen before. It's ... different. Dark.

Or maybe it's just how the light is hitting him. I blow him a kiss and back out of the driveway, careful to remember that the trailer pulling the car will go in the opposite direction. Like a good dad, he taught me how to back up a trailer and a boat, so I don't need the help of a man.

With one last honk goodbye, I drive down the road and sigh. It's liberating. I'm so excited to have my own place and to make my way in the world. Right now, I work at a little lingerie/evening gown boutique in town, but what I really want to do, if I ever have the guts to do it, is sing.

Not for a big crowd. I'm not about that life. No way in hell. Just a small crowd, something intimate, but that's just a fantasy. They call dreams, dreams for a reason. I'll never have the guts to go on stage. For now, I'll fantasize while I hang up beautiful luxurious lingerie and daydream about wearing the elegant gowns that get delivered.

It's only a ten-minute drive to my new apartment. It's away from the main Vegas strip, which is what I wanted because the strip gets so busy. I smile when I see the pale-yellow building with a bright blue roof. It's more of a one-bedroom house than it is an apartment; it's the size of a freaking shoe box. It does have a small fenced in yard, white shutters, and a blue door to match the roof. It's nice and perfect for me. I love bright colors. They make me happy. Things that are dark and dangerous freak me out.

I check my watch and debate how much I want to unpack tonight. Maybe I'll just pull out my mattress so I have something to sleep on, then run to go get some food since the sun will only be out for another hour. I love Vegas sunsets. The sky gets so orange with pinks mixed in, and I can watch the sun sink under the vast desert while I sit on my porch and have a glass of wine.

Yeah, being on my own is a beautiful thing.

I get out of the truck, take my car off the trailer, which takes up most of the hour I had, and by the time I have it on the ground, I'm sweating, and my dress is sticking to my skin. I wipe my forehead and exhale when I lift the truck door up. The rumble of the metal sliding back slowly shows me all my belongings.

My hands grip the sides of the mattress, and I plant my feet on the floor of the truck, grunting with all my might, but the damn thing doesn't move an inch.

"Oh, come on," I groan and try again. I yank and tug until I lose my breath and fall against it. "Okay!" I put my hands on my hips to relax a bit. I'm out of shape. I need to work out. Holy crap, Dad is right, I can't do this all by myself. I'm naïve to think I can carry a mattress all alone. I kick the thick fluffy bed, and it falls on the ground, flat.

"Huh," I say to myself when an idea hits me. I'll just sleep in the truck tonight. It will be safe enough. I'll get the battery-operated lamp out, and everything will be fine. If my dad finds out, he'll kill me. It's like camping, right? I'll be fine.

I plop my butt down on the mattress, and the big burning orb of the sun peeks over the edge of the sand. Sitting down was a mistake. My body falls backward, and I moan when the aches in my back tense at first. The pain fades, and exhaustion makes my lids flutter. While I'm laying here, I think about how I should have moved.

Dad, once again, is right.

I didn't need a damn trailer for my car. It was a waste of money. My dad offered to drive the truck while I drove the car behind him, but no, my stubborn, independent ass had to make everything difficult.

I'll never hear the end of it from him. He'll say, 'I told you so' and remind me of this for a few months, give me a hard time, and it will be all for fun.

My stomach grumbles, telling me I need to eat. Instead of driving like I had planned, I take my phone out and order from my favorite sushi place, Rho on Postmates, and wait. I bring my legs to my chest, wrap my arms around my knees, and lay my cheek against my thigh, watching the last rays of the sunset. I'm addicted to the beauty of it. It's so natural, and nothing can ever replicate it.

That little feeling of loneliness tickles my heart as I stare ahead, always impressed by the vast desert before me. It isn't the kind of loneliness where I miss my dad; it's the loneliness someone feels when they haven't experienced being in love before. I want to share this experience with someone. I want to hold hands and enjoy the simple things, like the sunset, like the stars, and make memories.

Maybe what I want is a dream too; maybe love doesn't exist for me. I love myself enough to enjoy being alone, but who genuinely wants to be alone when they can share a kiss, a home, and create a family, make memories?

I'm being naïve.

Again.

That isn't in the cards for some people, and maybe I need to let go of the dream of being someone's someone. All I'll ever need is myself, but the want, damn, the want for something bigger than myself is nearly consuming.

"Ah, I have an order for Juliette?" a man knocks on the side of the truck. "The person said to come to the big red truck."

"That's me!" I jump up and walk to the edge where I can step down onto the road. "Thank you so much." I take the plastic bag from him that contains all my yummy goodies and the Coke he has in his hand.

"Moving in?"

"Yep," I say a little too cheery. "Sorry, I'm excited."

He chuckles, brushing his fingers over his lips. He's good looking with his dirty blond hair and light scruff on his face. He's wearing a polo and khakis, a bit frat boy for my taste, but I wouldn't say no to a date with him. "No worries. I felt the same when I got my first place. Have a good night, I'll see you around."

"Bye," I say softly, watching him jog back to his car. Of course, he doesn't want to date me. I look wrecked, and he probably likes bikini models. I'm not overweight, but I have big boobs and thick thighs to carry around all the junk in my trunk. I do have a tiny waist due to the ab routine I do three times a week.

I take out the lamp from the box labeled 'random stuff' and turn it on, enjoying my sushi in peace. A coyote howls in the distance, signaling the pack its location.

If only I had my own pack then maybe I wouldn't be sitting in a truck by myself on the outskirts of Vegas.

It is dangerous.

I can be really dumb sometimes. I'm too eager, too impulsive. Everything has to be now, now, now. If I'd taken a minute to think about this move, I would have done it all differently.

I toss my container to the side and lay on the mattress, hoping tomorrow will be a better day. I just have to survive the night.

Hopefully, coyotes don't find me and eat me. The last thing I want is to be a toothpick for a wild animal.

"Yeah?" I answer the phone while I'm tightening a new oil filter. I'm currently underneath an old Buick, and I swear, the owner doesn't know that the oil needs to be changed every three-thousand miles on an old car like this. The oil was sludge, like a big hunk of Jell-O. I don't know how the old man let it get like that, but he better be glad he didn't ruin the engine.

"I'll open the gate," I say with more of a bite than usual. I'm the only one working today, well with Tank on the tow truck. Other than that, all the other guys are on a run for the Prez. Usually I lead the way on runs, but not this time. When Reaper gives an order, I follow it, and he told me to stay here. I don't mind. My mind is cloudy, and I'm frustrated I haven't found a place for the club I want to open. My good idea is slowly going down the drain.

I only want to be helpful for the club. I thought this was a way to repay Reaper for everything he's done for me. I also owe him for knocking Sarah across the jaw—it was an accident—a punishment he has yet to give me. I'm not looking forward to. Whatever it is, it's going to fucking hurt.

Planting my boots on the ground, I push off the stained cement and roll out from under the car. Standing, I grab the black towel, that used to be white but now is stained from oil, and wipe my hands off. I see Tank, one of our Prospects, driving down the dirt road, a truck on the flatbed.

I step into the raging morning heat and tuck the rag into my back pocket as Tank brings the truck to a stop. Tank is a huge fucker, pure muscle, and he looks like he's squeezed into a tin can right now. He looks mean as hell, but the guy is the softest damn thing since the stuffed teddy bear was invented.

"Hey, Tank, what ya got for me?" I shout to him as he hops down from the driver's side.

Tank walks around the front and tucks his hands in his back pocket as he kicks rocks along the driveway before going to the panel that lowers the flatbed to the ground. "Um, I got a…"

I lean forward to hear what he has to say, but he's so damn soft spoken that I can't hear a thing. "Prospect, speak the hell up," I order him, and his eyes widen with a tinge of fear. His throat bobs as he gulps ,and then he nods.

"It was parked in a no parking zone," he whispers and then clicks the button to lower the bed to the ground.

"Alright." I head for the back of the truck and notice by the logo on the back door it's a moving truck. Damn it, this isn't good. Someone is going to raise hell when they realize their shit is missing. Maybe there's something in the back that will tell me who to call. This shouldn't have been towed, but I'm not going to tell Tank that. He'll get all gloomy, and I don't feel like dealing with gloomy. I'm gloomy enough. I need something bright and cute.

Maybe I do need a dog. At least the dog will be happy to see me every day, and what's better than that?

I grip the rusted metal handle and turn it to the left then lift, letting it roll back. My eyes adjust for a quick second into the dark space, and then the sunlight trickles in, revealing a figure laying on the mattress. "Shit!" In one leap I hop inside, hurrying to the person's side. They might need help.

I expect to see blood, bruises, tears, and a story of something bad because that's what always lands on the Ruthless doorstep, but when I get to their side, I find the prettiest woman I've ever laid my eyes on.

She's in a blue sundress, but I can't see the rest of her body due to a blanket covering her. Her hands lay on her stomach as she sleeps. I can't believe she didn't wake up as Tank towed her. I bet she can sleep through a bomb going off, which isn't a good thing. What if he hadn't been Tank but someone else who towed her, or worse—stole the truck with her inside? She didn't think her plan through, and that pisses me off.

My anger quickly flees when I see her big tits pressing against her dress, the smooth curves of her cleavage teasing me. Her skin is pale and creamy, and her dark brown hair is tied in a knot on top of her head. Her lashes are long, thick, and casts shadows onto the top of her plump cheeks. She lets out a soft sigh, and her lips part.

Jesus Christ, it's the prettiest fucking sound I've ever had the pleasure of hearing.

My eyes lock onto her mouth, and my cock threatens to awaken, pressing against the zipper of my pants. Her lips are carved from sin, promising nothing but pleasure, and I'm dying to be the sinner who gets a taste.

She starts to wiggle, and then her arms lift above her head as she stretches. The mystery woman rubs her eyes and yawns, a little squeak leaving her throat as she tries to wake up. Damn it, she's so hot and cute all at the same time, and I know if I put my hands on her, I'll just dirty her up with all of my darkness and wicked ways.

A woman like this deserves the best. I'm not good enough for her. She's clean against my greased-up skin, and even in the stuffy box of the moving truck, I can smell her mango shampoo. I'll taint her with my sweat from a long day's work. She deserves a pretty boy to match her appearance, but the thought has the monster I keep locked away roaring forward.

And it's determined to get her filthy.

Her lashes flutter open, slowly blinking as she wakes up to the world, gracing us with her presence.

My god, her eyes are the color of the sea, but not blue, no, her eyes are sea green, reminding me of the beach in the tropics. When she sees me, she smiles, and the weight on my chest lifts off like it was never there to begin with.

But then, it hits her that a strange man is hovering over her, admiring her.

Her body too, but she doesn't need to know that bit.

Yet.

She grabs the blanket, brings it to her chest, and scrambles backward until her back hits the boxes behind her. She lets out an ear-piercing scream that bounces off the metal walls of the truck.

I wince but hold my hands out to show her I'm no threat. "I know, alright. You're safe here. Okay? You're at Kings' Garage. Your truck got towed for being parked in a no parking zone. It's okay. You're free to go whenever you want. I promise, you're safe."

"Kings' Garage?" she asks, and her voice is so light with a soft rasp. I imagine her humming around my cock while she sucks me between those plump red lips. "Ruthless Kings?" Her eyes get wide with fear and suddenly pool with tears. "You're going to kill me."

"What?" I cock my head to the side from her ridiculous question. "I'm not going to kill you." I've killed before, but she doesn't need to know that. "You're safe here. Ruthless Kings don't hurt women."

"That's not what my dad says. You better let me go. You don't want trouble."

"Woman, did you hear me? I said you were free to go

whenever you want." I stand and jump down from the inside of the truck, leaving her on the mattress. I hardly know her, and she's already a bigger pain in my ass than Poodle. She isn't listening to me, and I can't stand it when people don't fucking listen.

"Hey! Don't walk away from me." Her voice gets hard and fierce. It reminds me of a chihuahua getting all worked up. It's adorable. "I'm not scared of you." She shoves my back, and instinctively I reach for the screwdriver I keep at my ear and turn around, placing it right under her chin.

"That's foolish of you to say," I whisper, looking her up and down. Her dress is dangerous, showing all her curves, and she's wearing heels. When the hell did she put those devilish things on? Fuck me, they're making her legs defined, and now I'm imagining flipping her dress over and fucking her right here while she stands in those stiletto pumps.

Jesus, the woman is dangerous.

"I thought you said you didn't hurt women." She juts her chin out against the tip of the screwdriver. If she's scared, she isn't showing it like she did in the truck. She's strong, has a backbone.

I love that.

"I don't," I say, refusing to tell her the way I want to hurt her will only last a second as I fill her pretty pussy up with my big cock. We stay there like that for a few minutes, staring into each other's eyes longer than normal. I'm reacting to her in ways I've kept locked away for a long time.

Love isn't real, only hate is. I chant the mantra in my head, but the more I look at her, the more the words fade. I look away and sit back on the slider and then disappear under the Buick I no longer need to work on. I can pretend I am, so I don't have to talk to the little walking wet dream anymore.

She's driving me crazy. My cock is harder than it has ever been, straining against my jeans, and I don't want her to see it. She'll probably get disgusted that a guy like me finds a woman like her so attractive.

"Hey, I'm talking to you!" she huffs, and her heels kiss the ruined cement. It's almost comical that something so beautiful would grace these floors. I never thought I'd see the day, but here I am, witnessing a miracle with my own two eyes.

"I'm busy," I grunt, banging against the undercarriage of the car so it sounds like I'm doing something. "Hand me a socket wrench." I hold out my hand, waiting for her to place it in my hand. "Come on, woman. I don't have all day."

"My name is not woman. It's Juliette, you freaking caveman."

"Listen, princess," I start to say when she puts a tool in my hand, but I can tell by the weight and feel of it, it isn't the right thing. "It's not the right one. Give me a different one." I let the flat head screwdriver fall to the ground and hold out my hand again. "Listen, I don't really care about your huffy puffy attitude right now. I said you were free to go, no harm no foul. Climb in your truck and leave. You're the one making it difficult."

She plops another tool in my hand, and I sigh in frustration when I see it's small drill bit in my palm. Has this woman ever

45

seen a damn toolbox before? "That's not it either. Hand me—" I'm silenced when she jerks me out from under the car and lays the tip of her heel against my neck.

Juliette smirks down at me with her hands on her hip, looking sassy and sexy, and my eyes rake up her thick legs. The white edge of her lace panties tease me, and I want nothing more than to grab her calves and sit her on my face while I eat that sweet pussy.

My mouth waters, and my tongue twitches. Just one flick across her clit. That's all I'm asking for.

"Listen, princess," she spits my nickname at me, and it makes me smirk. She's feisty. "I'm not a mechanic. You want a pocket wrench—"

"Socket wrench," I correct her while she stares down at me.

"Whatever. You want tools given to you, get your mechanic."

"Why would I want one of my ugly mechanics when I have a pretty thing like you standing in my garage?" I whip back, and if I'm not mistaken, a blush tints her cheeks. A bit of the fight leaves her, and she breaks our gaze, glancing away from me.

Interesting. She'll give me lip all damn day, but one compliment renders her speechless. Mental. Note.

"I have moving to do," she says, removing the tip of her heel from my throat. She struts away, giving me a view of her wide lush hips that I want to hold onto.

Perfection.

I never thought it could exist in the back of a moving truck wearing a blue dress. She looks too fucking good as she places her heel on the step and lifts herself up into the driver's seat. She settles in, and I chuckle when I notice she can barely see over the wheel. She goes to crank it, but it just turns and turns until it dies. The engine starts to steam, and her mouth drops open before she hits her head against the steering wheel.

She climbs down, landing on her heels like a pro before stomping her way over to me. The steam fogs behind her as the wind blows a few pieces of her chocolate brown hair away from her face. With how her hips sway seductively, it's like something out of an action movie before the woman lets her hair down and shakes the strands loose.

Oh, please, take your hair down.

She doesn't. She stops in front of me with an angry scowl on her face.

"Looks like you're stuck with me," I tease.

"Yay me," she sounds all but enthused.

Sirens roar in the distance, and the annoyance in her eyes quickly turns to panic.

"What's wrong?" I ask her as I make my way over to the truck. "Just the cops."

"Crap, crap, crap," she says. "Oh, he's going to be pissed." Juliette paces and brings her thumb between her lips and nibbles.

I walk over and slap her hand out of her mouth. "Don't do that. It's a gross habit."

"Says the guy covered in oil."

Right. The guy covered in oil is a low-life and gross. Good

to know.

"I didn't mean it like that," she says in an apologetic tone when she realizes her mistake.

The sirens pull up to the garage, and two cop cars skid to a stop. Reaper comes out of the side door, walking in quick strides over me.

"What did you do?" he asks.

"I don't fucking know. Nothing!" I don't think I did…

"It's not either of you. It's me." Her sweet voice wraps around my heart, and I can't believe for one damn minute this girl is a criminal. I've met criminals. She isn't one of them. Criminals don't look that good. Facts.

"Juliette!" Sheriff Fuckwad Johnson yells from behind his open driver's side door as he aims his weapon at me. "Get back from these thugs."

"Dad. I'm fine. It's all a big misunderstanding. The truck won't start, see?" Juliette points to the truck that's still smoking.

"Juliette, get over here now," the sheriff orders, and I can tell she's embarrassed because her eyes shine with tears. She closes her eyes, takes a deep breath, and opens them again, and that strong resolve is back. Juliette throws her shoulders back, spins on her heel, and walks toward her dad. "Put her in the car," he says to his deputy before walking over to me and Reaper, gun back in his holster, but his hand is still on it.

I bet his finger is just twitching to pull that trigger. We aren't fans of the sheriff. He's a dirty cop, and we're never on the same page. He wants to tear the club down and kick us out of the city, but we aren't going anywhere.

Ever.

"You better stay away from my daughter. She's too good to be seen around low-lifes like you," he sneers and then spits on our boots.

I growl, taking a step forward. No one disrespects the Prez like that. Reaper's palm slaps against my chest, stopping me from shoving my screwdriver between his eyes. A skill I've honed in on over the years.

"We will deliver the truck after it's fixed, Sheriff," Reaper says calmly, but I can tell he's about to lose it.

"I'll have a deputy pick it up. I don't want you knowing where my daughter lives." With that, he turns and walks away, slamming the door after he cranks the car and flips off his lights.

Juliette turns to look out the back window as they drive away, and something in my gut clenches with how she stares at me.

"Remember that punishment, Tool?"

Fuck. "Yes, Prez." I'm ready. I've been waiting on this day for months.

Reaper turns on his heel, nose to nose with me. "You're not to touch the sheriff's daughter. We don't need that mess on our doorstep. Do I make myself clear?" he threatens. If I don't stay away, nothing good will happen to me. "I saw that look you two just shared. You can have anyone else in this city, but not her. Stay. The. Fuck. Away." He shoves a finger in the middle of my chest and makes his way inside the clubhouse, slamming the door.

This should be easy, but I find myself wishing he would've carved a heart in my chest instead. I don't want anyone else. I want her.

The off-limits sheriff's daughter.

The woman in blue.

The woman who sounds like a song sparrow.

Disobeying the Prez means death, but hearing heaven might be worth it if it's in the sound of her voice.

Juliette is the sin in my world of evil, and I'm going to fail at being the saint Reaper wants me to be.

My dad is furious at me. He has every reason to be, but it's not like I asked to be at Kings' Garage. I fell asleep. I didn't know I'd get towed!

That argument didn't work on my father. He gave me a lecture on the Ruthless Kings and told me just how ruthless they were, how dangerous and violent. He told me about cases could possibly forever be open because they can't find the bodies of the men the Ruthless Kings have killed. My dad had a wild look in his eyes, one that told me he was on the verge of mania.

I haven't heard from him since.

Which means I'm getting the silent treatment.

He made good on his word. My things were delivered by movers early this morning and were waiting for me at my tiny home, according to his text message. Since I had nowhere to stay, I stayed with Dad last night.

I woke up to an empty house because Dad was being a dramatic brat. I decided to walk home since my car was there, and I had no other options.

Now, I find myself sweating again in this dress, that I've somehow worn for three days now, and I'm disgusted with myself. How has this happened? Who gets towed to a damn garage while sleeping?

And who also meets the hottest man they have ever seen in their life? Whewie, that man is sex on a stick. He oozes the sexy bad-boy biker vibe with all those tattoos. I mean, he is covered in them, head to freaking toe. Even the sides of his temples are tattooed. Half of his head is shaved while the other half is pitch black and long in length, hanging to his chin. On top of that, he has a thick beard that I want to run my fingers through and bury my nose in. I bet he takes care of it with beard oil that smells so good, it will make me want to straddle his lap and have my way with him.

My body flushes when I remember his body against mine when he put that screwdriver under my chin. I knew he wouldn't hurt me, but the feeling of danger with a man who exudes power so naturally has my nipples tightening and my clit throbbing. A man like him probably has women left and right. He'll want nothing to do with me.

That doesn't mean I can't take care of myself to the thoughts of him. And as soon as I get home, I'll do exactly that.

I'm drenched in sweat by the time I get to my house. My feet are killing me. I took off my heels two blocks ago, and I can't wait to soak in a hot bubble bath. I groan when I make my way up the stairs. My shoulders sting from the sun, and a hint of red on my skin tells me I have officially sunburned.

I always make sure to wear sunscreen, but the events that have happened over the last few days have left my mind a mess. A new welcome mat greets me, and when I look down, I know that's where Dad put the house key. I squat and flip over the mat then take the shiny silver key in hand. I stand and slide it into the doorknob, slowly opening the blue door.

Air conditioning greets me, and I close my eyes, moaning as it dries the sweat on my skin and eases the ache on the flesh of my shoulders. I open my eyes and smile to myself as I toss my heels to the left. The dark hardwood floors shine, and my bare feet stick to the floor as I make my way to the bathroom. I reach around to grab the zipper of my dress and drag it down, but I freeze in place when I notice something off about the house.

Taking a step back, I look left noticing that my living room is unpacked and my green Victorian couch sets against the wall across from the windows that have a built-in bench, the perfect reading nook. I hurry to the right where the kitchen is and open each cabinet. All of my pots and pans are put away.

My pink retro coffeepot is plugged up next to the sink, and I blink away tears of relief. Not because my house is unpacked, but because it's my dad's doing. I thought he might have hated me for ending up at Kings' Garage. I notice a note on the counter, and I

53

take two steps forward, picking the square paper up.

It's from my dad. He always uses the small notebook that can be slid in his uniform pocket.

Pumpkin,

Fridge is stocked, pantry is full, house is set up; except the clothes in your bedroom. I love you.

Dad

I gasp and hurriedly open the fridge doors to see all of my favorite foods and drinks. I pull out my phone from my dress pocket—yes, my dress has pockets; it's awesome, I know—and send him a quick thank you text.

The only way this house could have been unpacked so quick is if he had a few deputies here too. I hold the note to my chest and skip down the hall toward the bathroom that's attached to my bedroom. It's the one room that sold this place to me. My heart fell in love with the classic claw-foot tub and walk-in shower. It has a double vanity sink that's a bit outdated, but I don't mind putting some love into it.

My dress falls to the floor of my bedroom, and I step out of it and lean against the wall as I stare at my new bathroom. Everything is set up in here too. My favorite lotions, perfumes, shampoos. Everything.

I have the best dad in the world.

The walls have an awful rose wallpaper on them that I plan on getting rid of as soon as possible; it's hideous. My hands grip the sleek gold handles of hot and cold, turning them equally to create a nice temperature. I plug the tub with the gold stopper and then pour my mango-scented bubble bath under the rush of water. I'm addicted to anything that smells like mangos.

But I don't like the fruit. I don't know why.

I sink into the water and groan, lean my head against the edge, and let my arms fall to the bottom of the tub on either side of me. The warm water heals my body. It's been a hell of a few days, and I want to relax.

Shutting my eyes, the biker's face comes to view. I never got his name, but I bet it's something sexy; it has to be when a man looks as good as he does. His eyes are so dark they blend to the edge of black. It's like looking into pools of ink or oil, which fits since his life is based around it.

I remember how he smelled. Sure, there's sweat and grime, but underneath all that, I remember pine.

He reminds me of a demon ready to possess my body. If I allow the hijack to happen, I'll succumb to his dark and delicious ways, and I have a feeling I'll never want to walk on the safe side again. I'll be the Persephone to his Hades, but the ride will be a far cry from hell.

My hands find my breasts and the hard, beaded nipples that ache for his touch burn between my fingers as I pinch and roll them. I whimper into the empty bathroom and imagine what he looks like naked. I bet he is all hard lines and abs. The tattoos on his neck disappear under his shirt, and I want to lick every black line on his body.

While one hand keeps a tight hold on my nipple, my free hand moves between my legs, sliding over the tuft of hair over my pussy. My fingers glide through my folds, and my hole clenches and flexes with the need to be filled. I press my fingers inside my aching body, and my entire body heats.

And it isn't from the water.

I pump my fingers vigorously in and out of my virgin hole, curling my fingers at the last second to hit that special spot that intensifies my orgasm. My clit is sensitive, but I've never been able to get off by rubbing it. I have to have something inside me. It's why I have a collection of toys. There isn't a better feeling than being filled up and stretched.

"Yes," I groan, sliding a third finger in, and my hips push down, seeking more than I can give myself. I bet hot-biker man can give me exactly what I need. I imagine him sliding his cock inside me and breaking that damn barrier I hate so much. I'll finally become a woman. He won't go easy on me. It will be hard with grit and maybe an edge of pain.

He looks like the kind of man who carries too much power to hide the amount of force he can bring to the bedroom. I want to be on the devastating end of it—wrung out, gasping, body shaking as he pulls orgasm after mind-blowing orgasm from my body.

Like no man ever has.

He'll know how to have his way with me, and I'll let him.

I bite my bottom lip when my lower belly tightens, and the weightless feeling numbs my limbs. I'm seconds away from having the best orgasm of my life.

I fuck myself faster, harder, thrusting my hips down and causing the water to splash over the sides of the tub, soaking the floor. I don't care. I need this. I'm right there. I need more. The quick fantasy in my mind has him shooting his cum deep inside me, conquering me, and making me his.

My orgasm slams against my bones, igniting fireworks in my eyes, blinding me for a few seconds as the shocks of pleasure tingle the tips of my toes to the abused flesh on my lip. I keep my fingers inside me when I fall limp, gasping for breath, and I pretend my fingers are his cock still enjoying me.

"Oh wow," I say, a bit blitzed and drunk off my orgasm. When the bath becomes cold, I pull my hand free and turn the hot water knob again to warm the water. Hot biker guy is a man I'll never see again, except in my dreams, and even though my heart is still pumping in wild abandon, the thought of not even knowing his name makes the high come crashing down.

My dad will make sure the Ruthless Kings are never in my life. I can't go against my father, not the man who raised me, who has been there for me twenty-four-seven after my mother died. He hasn't even taken care of himself. He's focused on me and only me. If he doesn't want me mingling with the Ruthless Kings, I can at least grant his wish.

I never thought the one thing I'd be forbidden to do would be the thing I want most. That's how it works, though. Anything someone can get on a day-to-day basis isn't special; it's normal, and there isn't an urge.

When something is out of reach, out of the norm and forbidden? It only makes the urge spike to a dangerous level.

I've never disobeyed my father and I've never had a rebellious streak, but biker man is already bringing it out of me, like a damn magnet, bringing to the surface all the wants I've denied myself.

He's the forbidden fruit, and I want to take the biggest, juiciest bite out of him. I know he will ruin me. The temptation is sardonic, wrapping and constricting around the purity of my soul to replace my innocence.

How can a girl resist?

It's the fifth place I've looked at with the real estate agent, and I've hated every single one she has shown me. They're fucking dives, and I'm starting to wonder if she thinks we can't afford more than this. Bullseye is being a grouch, and he looks a bit pale. He's holding the spot on his chest where he got shot, and I'm wondering if we need to call it a day and head back to the house. I have to meet with Skirt anyway about the house, then there is church later tonight about some cookout Reaper wants to hold for all the chapters.

All. Of. Them.

That's about two-hundred people and a beacon for the sheriff to come to our property and make things more difficult.

"So what do you think?" Amber or Amy or whatever the hell her name is asks in a preppy, cheerleader voice, and it grinds on my nerves. She's wearing an expensive silk skirt with a plain blouse. She's too skinny, and with how she's looking at me, I can tell she wants me. It's too bad. She isn't my type.

I like my meat a bit thicker and off-limits.

Juliette.

Damn, just the thought of her name gets my cock worked up.

"I think it's a shithole, lady," Bullseye growls, toying with a metal dart in his hand, and by his body language, he's a breath away from throwing it at her. "It ticks me off that you're showing us these dumps in bad neighborhoods. We told you we were good for it, so why do you keep testing us?" He grips the dart with so much force he snaps it in half.

Before the situation gets out of control, like having to figure out how to dispose of a body, I diffuse the situation with my charm; something Bullseye lacks.

"I think what my friend means to say is—"

"I said what I fucking meant," Bullseye interrupts me and stands, leaning against the bar as he points at the real estate agent. "You heard me, why?"

She jumps in her expensive heels and licks her lips. She tries to speak but looks like fear has disabled her vocal cords. "I'm sorry. I was only following instruction," she whispers.

I tilt my head, letting her words roll around a bit as I think. "Instruction? From whom?"

"The sheriff. He found out you were looking for a place on the strip, and he wanted me to show you the worst. Please, don't hurt me. I'll…" She ran up to Bullseye and rubbed her hands along his chest. "I'll do anything."

"Anything?" he grunts.

"Yes." She nods in quick bobs.

"So if I said bend over and lift that skirt so I can have my way with your pussy, you would?"

Damn it, Bullseye. Why did I bring him with me again?

She tries to take a step back from him. "I—um, I—" she stutters, and Bullseye grabs her wrists gently, tugging her to him again.

"Listen, don't come onto me unless you're willing to go through with it. If that's all, leave. We don't have time to waste with shit like this," Bullseye gently pushes her away from him, and she rights her blouse. Her face is red, flushed with embarrassment, and I'm assuming terror.

"Want to let you know, though, doing us wrong doesn't get you any favors with the club. Go against the sheriff, show us a good spot, and we will be in debt to you."

"In debt? Like, you'll owe me a favor?" she replies to me.

"Only me. So if you need anything, ask for Tool when you call the clubhouse, okay, Amber?"

"It's Amy," she corrects me, and I want to roll my eyes.

"Great." I look around this dump again and cringe. I hear the scuffle of rats inside the walls. The floor is rotted, the roof is caved in with water damage, and there's a smell in that not even a fire can get rid of. "Can we go?"

"Of course." She hurries by us, and Bullseye leans forward

and bites the air, making her screech and walk faster in front of us.

He laughs, and I slap his shoulder, making him grunt with pain. "Stop being an ass," I warn him. "You don't want me to tell Prez."

"You don't want me to tell Prez," he mocks me like a child. "What are you, a snitch?"

"What are you? Twelve? Jesus, Bullseye, get to walking to the truck. And stay in the truck for the next place we see. I don't feel like dealing with your ornery ass."

"I don't feel like dealing with your ornery ass," he mimics again, and I slap him on the back of the head before he gets into the passenger seat of the truck, arms crossed just like a kid would be.

I slam the passenger door and take a deep breath, telling myself not to stab him between the eyes. Don't do it. Don't do it. Calm down.

The sun bears down on my eyes causing me to squint as I run around the truck. I gaze into the windshield and see Bullseye flicking me off. When we get to the clubhouse, I'm going to have Doc tranquilize him so everyone can get a break from Bullseye.

I crank the truck, ignoring Bullseye as he mumbles under his breath. I pull forward and follow Amy's small red convertible down the strip. Building by building, I can tell we're finally getting into a better area. The prostitutes get less and less until they are finally non-existent. The sun shines brighter, and tourists walk on the sidewalks pointing to each impressive building they see, like the Bellagio.

This is better.

She turns her blinker on and turns into a garage. It's so much cooler in here than it is outside since it's shaded. I lean against the headrest for a second, enjoying the absence of the sun, when Bullseye opens his big mouth. "Are you really making me stay in the car?"

He sounds so sad it's almost comical.

"No. Keep your mouth shut around Amy. You're being an ass."

"Yes, sir," he says, sounding forlorn like a pouty kid.

We get out of the truck, and our boots land on the parking lot floor with a hard thud, bouncing off the cement walls along with Amy's high heels. She still seems flustered as we walk toward her and keeps her head down.

This cop is getting involved in matters that he has nothing to do with, and that's a problem. Sheriff Johnson just got elected, and he seems to have zeroed in on us. I don't like it. He doesn't want us coming to the strip, why? He has nothing on us that proves we're dangerous to society. Is it implied?

Maybe.

But if there's no proof, then Sheriff is harassing us, and it's not something I like one bit.

"About the place," Amy starts to speak, pulling me from my murderous thoughts of hanging the sheriff by his neck. "It used to be an Italian restaurant, but the owner died in a terrible hotel explosion. Can you believe that?" She shakes her head in sadness. "I hope he died quickly."

Bullseye and I share a look, knowing it's the same explosion that put Reaper on his ass and Moretti in a coma.

"Shame," we say at the same time.

"Anyway, it's a pretty big place—bar, stage, and all that jazz. Location is great. Right in the heart of Vegas. It needs a few repairs because it's been empty, but it's beautiful. It just needs a little love." She grunts when she pulls the door open after unlocking the knob. A cloud of smoke puffs in her face, and she coughs, waving her hand to get the dust out of her eyes. "Like I said, it's been awhile."

"Little dust never killed nobody. I don't mind cleaning," I say as I step inside the place that hopefully is my future. It's dark, and I can hardly see anything. A light buzz sounds, and a second later the lights come on. I'm taken aback.

It's perfect.

It's narrow more than it is wide, but it goes way back.

Bullseye whistles. "Holy shit, Tool. This place is fancy." I hear the awe in his voice, and he looks up at the ceiling, staring at the large chandeliers hanging.

Yeah, those have got to go if I get his place.

The place has been cleared out of all the tables and booths besides a few chairs. A thick coat of dust lays on the floor, and our boots leave tracks as we walk deeper into the empty space.

"To the right, you have a bar made of a hundred-year-old

wood. It's original, just like the floors. The previous owner wanted to make sure he kept something traditional." Amy explains some of the history, and for the first time, I'm actually interested in learning about something that happened in the past.

"To the left we have the stage. Oh, wait, you can't see it because of the curtain. Let me figure out how to move it." Amy walks to the side where a big gold rope is, reminding me of something that should be attached to a bell, waiting for someone to tug to sound the loud ring.

"This place is nice, Tool," Bullseye says. "Can you afford—"

I snap my head to him and narrow my eyes to tell him he better not say another word about money.

I have plenty.

I've saved up while doing a few favors for the Prez and other clubs. Let's just say, the loose ends I take care of never speak again. No one knows that except Reaper, and it's better to keep it that way. It's one of the few illegal activities that is necessary. If there's a problem, I take care of it.

Not even Bullseye, our Sergeant at Arms, knows. He should. He can clean up with me, and we would make one hell of a team, but Reaper wants to keep it on the downlow. The more people who know, means the more people who talk, and talk means gossip.

"It's nice." I twist my head left and right, nodding in appreciation as I look at the old trim along the walls. For an Italian place, I wondered if the owner knew he had Irish crescents carved in the wood lining the ceiling. I can imagine it now. Small private booths will line the front of the stage, reserved for VIP only. Other tables will be first come first serve, and the bar will have stools for more seating. No room for dancing, well, not club dancing, just slow dance to enjoy the music being played. I'm thinking old school, like blues or R&B.

The curtain, instead of rising, falls and crashes against the floor, and Amy lets out a scream, and another wave of foggy dust hides her.

"Woman is a damn mess," Bullseye says, watching as she stumbles onto the stage, coughs, and spreads her arms out.

"Ta-da," she says with a smile, revealing a stage made for maybe four people.

"She's cute," Bullseye chuckles, appreciating Amy's showmanship.

"Don't even think about it. The real estate agent is off-limits, Bullseye. Don't make this difficult."

"I can't fuck anyway," he grumbles. "Hurts my chest and lungs. I just got those bitches drained from moving too quickly. I'm not doing it again. Getting a tube shoved in your side isn't pleasant."

His healing process has been slow, but the doctors say it's normal when they have to crack a chest. The body is never the same after that. And I can see the toll it's taking on him.

"What do you guys think?" Amy's voice is like nails on a chalkboard for me. I bring my gaze to hers to see her in the same 'ta-da' position.

"I love it so far. Can I see the kitchen?" She runs off the stage, her hands up as she takes small steps to not trip.

"Come with me. It's in the back through this door." Amy almost falls on her face from coming down the steps, but she catches herself, tugging the end of her skirt to pull it down her legs. She smooths her palms down her thighs, pulling herself together.

She's cute, but Bullseye is right; she's a fucking mess too.

Amy opens the door to the back, which I decide immediately has to go. I want big double swinging doors. Having a door here makes this place look like a house too much. The kitchen has red tile floors, older appliances, and a few cobwebs here and there.

"The fridge needs replaced and so does the oven. But the space is large—" Amy begins to explain, but I interrupt her.

"I'll take it. Let's go back to your office and sign papers. I can pay you today. Cash."

"Damn, fuck you for making me pay for drinks last night," Bullseye complains and knocks his fist on a hanging pot, which has a domino effect. The chain hanging on the wall creaks then cracks, and the pots shake and clink together before falling onto the island.

It's loud, and the ringing of pots and pans, metal against metal, has my brains shaking and ears ringing. "You're paying for that," I tell him.

"What?" he yells over a piece of ceiling falling next.

I roll my eyes and turn around, ready to get the hell of here and sign the contract so I can get to work. My foot breaks through one of the floorboards and I yank it out, scuffing my boots in the process. Damn it, these are brand new. I'll have to polish them later.

My shoulder presses against the door, and I swing it open and step out in the hot sun. Two things I notice immediately. Across the street is a lingerie store, and Juliette is in the window hanging a new piece of sexy lace on a mannequin that I can see her wearing for me.

Only Sheriff Fuckwad is leaning against the club truck, arms crossed with a pissed off look on his face. "Don't pinch your brows, Sheriff, you'll get wrinkles, but I guess that wouldn't matter for your ugly mug."

Bullseye and Amy come out of the building next, and my club brother is right next to me, ready to fight. I don't know how he will, but the effort is what counts. The sheriff gives Amy a dangerous look, one that has every instinct in me rising up and ready to kill.

"Thought I gave you an order, Amy."

"Um, I'll be emailing you the paperwork," Amy says to me before running to her car, scared as hell. The kind of panic you see when someone is afraid for their life. Is that what the sheriff is doing? Threatening whoever comes within five feet of us?

"You won't be opening anything here, Logan," he sneers my name, and I clench my jaw together. This asshole reminds me of my father, and I know how that ended. I was the victor.

I came out on top.

I do every time.

I peer over his shoulders to see Juliette staring at me with her pretty lips open in an O. I lift my hand and wave to the woman I want more than my next breath. "Sheriff, there isn't anything you can do to stop me. Let's go, Bullseye." I go to make my way around the truck to get to the driver's side, and the sheriff stops me, palm on my chest and his free hand on his gun.

"You better stay away from her. She isn't for you," he spits, pushing me to the left before going back to his cruiser. He reverses and purposely backs into the front of the truck, denting the grill, and pulls away.

"Fucking asshole," Bullseye sneers and hops into the truck.

He is. I can deal with asshole. What I can't deal with is an asshole with bad intentions. She isn't for me? What does that mean?

If she isn't for me, who is she meant for?

So I don't like an empty house. It's too quiet. It's how I ended up at the humane society, ready to adopt a dog. Plus, having a dog will bring me security, a sense of safety if an attacker breaks into the house.

I slam the door to my car and tilt my head back onto my shoulders. Holy mother of sour patch straws, it's sprinkling. It never rains. It's hot, dry, and I'll even see a tumbleweed now and again. Rain? It's a sweet, precious thing that we locals never see enough of. The first light sprinkle on my skin makes me grin.

I stand in the middle of the parking lot, spread my arms, and stand there as I let the rain fall on me. It's coming down a little heavier now, not enough to bounce off my skin, but enough for me to feel the small droplets roll down my arm. No one understands how rare it is to feel rain when you live in the desert. It's like experiencing a miracle, one that you actually get to touch and feel.

"Little sparrow, you should know better than to stand like that in the rain."

A voice I've dreamed about over the last few nights makes my body tighten with shock and lust. I didn't expect to see him again. Vegas isn't the smallest city, and how he and I met, well, that was completely out of the norm. So color me shocked that when I turn around, I see his sexy, handsome biker face.

He has on a black tank top that matches the depth of his hair, and it's suctioned to his body because his muscles are so big. I can see the indentations of his abs and the swells of his pecs. My mouth drools on itself until I'm swallowing a gallon of spit. Gross. Crap, is it dripping down my chin? I lift my hand and scratch my neck then work my way up to my chin to make sure I'm not making a complete fool of myself.

"It's raining," I say to him. Duh, Juliette. Way to be lame.

"I see that. You're enjoying it." His eyes roam down my body and back up to my face, and that's when I realize my nipples are hard and my dress is sticking to my skin. I cross my arms over my chest, and the rain starts to come down harder, thunder rolling in the distance to tell us the storm is far from being over.

He wraps his arm around me and spins me toward the entrance of the humane society. "Come on, little sparrow. I don't want you to get sick being in the rain like this."

"Being in the rain doesn't make you sick. That's a myth." I let him guide me through the parking lot, and right as we're about to cross the small street separating the lot and the building, he holds me back to keep me from crossing. A speeding car ignores us completely and whizzes on by, splashing water on the both of us.

There's dirt in my mouth.

My dress has gone from damp to soaking freaking wet.

"Asshole!" the sexy biker roars at the car that just splashed murky water on us. "You okay, Juliette?" He cups my face gently, his eyes darting back and forth between mine. "I have a hoodie in my truck; let me grab it for you. Stay right here. Don't fucking move," he orders, pointing one finger to the ground where my feet are firmly planted.

"Okay," I whisper.

"I'm serious."

"I'm not moving!" I snap at his alpha dominate demand that makes me wet between the legs, but I want to fight him too.

His fingers slide under my chin, and he brings his lips down on mine in a quick, soft kiss that steals my breath and brain cells. "Good, I'd be heartbroken if you did," he says.

I just kissed a guy whose name I don't even know. He turns to walk toward his bike, but I grab his wrist, needing to know the name of the man who has me considering disappointing my father. "Who are you?" I ask, and he tugs his wrist free and gives me a sexy grin as he walks backward.

"You'd like to know that, wouldn't you?" The rain comes down harder now, and I can hardly see his body or hear his voice.

"It's why I asked!" What am I doing? I need to turn around,

go to my car, and leave. This man is dangerous. He probably picks his teeth with human bones or something and bathes in his victims' blood. That's what my dad tells me, but what if he's wrong? Maybe my dad was being dramatic to keep me away.

"Let's go," sex on a stick yells over the roar of the rain. His hand falls on my lower back as we run across the street. Safe under the awning, I run my hand over my face to get the water out of my eyes.

"Oh my gosh." I shake my head and then gather my hair in one hand, squeezing the water out of it, then I twist it up until it's a bun on top of my head.

"I hate to cover up that gorgeous body, but I bet you're cold." He tugs his sweatshirt over my head, and I nearly groan from how good the material smells. It's a black hoodie, of course, and it has 'Kings' Garage' labeled on the front of it, but it doesn't smell like a mechanic's garage. It smells like laundry detergent and pine. "You look good in my clothes," he says, sparking an arousal throughout my body. My breasts are heavy for his touch, and my clit throbs for his mouth.

"Don't get used to it, biker dude," I call him since I don't know his name.

"Biker dude? Biker dude!" His voice raises on a laugh. "I deserve that. I'm Tool."

"Tool?" I snort at the ridiculous, kind of hot nickname. It suits him, and it explains the reason for the screwdriver above his ear. "What's your real name?"

"Not a lot of people know it; why would I give it to you?" he asks, placing his hands on my hips to tug me to him when the doors to the animal shelter open, pulling me out of the way.

I smile at the people as they walk by and give Tool my attention. "Friends give each other the facts. I don't want to call you Tool."

He debates for a minute, rubbing his hand over the hair on his chin while he tries to figure me out. There's nothing to figure out. I want to get to know him more, even though I know I shouldn't.

"Logan." His voice deepens, wrapping around my body and bringing the hairs on my skin to stand up tall. I react to him in every way that can only get him into trouble with my father.

"Logan," I repeat, blinking up at him as I tilt my head back. "It's nice to meet you. Even if you are a pain in my ass."

He bends down, placing his lips next to my ear and his left hand on the side of my face. "The only pain you'll ever feel in your ass will be from my cock."

I gasp and rear back. No one has ever spoken to me like that. I have no idea what to say.

Logan laughs, places his hand on my lower back, and steers me inside. "Good. I know what shuts you up now."

"I'm going to shut you up if you don't watch it, biker dude!" I hiss at him, and since we're around people, he isn't able to do or say anything except growl.

And the growl does nothing but make my libido skyrocket more than it already was. I'm hanging on a dangerously thin thread. I'm tempted to push him in a closet and give in to the trouble he seems to bring to the surface.

Logan whispers into my ear, "I love it when you're feisty. It gets me all worked up."

My cheeks blush as we get to the counter, and the man behind the cash register is staring at me and smiling until he sees how soaked we are, and then the large happy grin falters. "Oh my goodness. You're wet to the core!" he says.

Yes, yes, I am. More than he will ever know.

"I'm fine." That's a lie if I've ever heard one. I need to get out of here and away from Logan. He isn't good for my rational mind.

"We are looking to adopt a dog," Logan says, making it sound like we're adopting one dog together.

I smile and shake my head. "What my friend here,"—he growls again—"is trying to say is we both are looking to adopt dogs. One for him, and one for me."

"Of course, oh how wonderful!" He claps his hands together and then hands us two clipboards with a sheet of paper on it. "Just fill out these questions, and we will get to you soon." The man behind the counter has a slender face with a smile too large for his lips. He has dark eyes, beady, and his skin has a natural pale glamour to it. A shiver wracks my body from the cold stare he gives me.

We take the clipboards and walk over to the chair lining the windows as we fill out our paper. I try to glance at his to see his responses, but he turns it away from me, as if I'm copying him and cheating like this is a test.

"Give me a break," I grumble, and the ball point of the pen makes the shape of my handwriting along the pages. Why do I want a dog? Do I have a yard? I understand that it takes six months for a dog to adjust to a new environment. Questions like that. Logan and I stand at the same time when we finish, and his tattooed arm brushes against mine. My lungs betray me, causing me to inhale a sharp breath from the quick, meaningless touch.

Is it meaningless? The touches we share. He makes my body come alive in ways that shouldn't be possible for any man to do to a woman. The want for him almost sends me to my knees.

Good thing I have strong legs. The only time I'll get on my knees is when—

"Excellent. Please follow me to where we keep the dogs."

Logan keeps his hand on my lower back, the heat from his palm sinking into the tight muscles around my spine. Is it possible to relax and be wound up at the same time? That's how I feel at the moment.

The guy opens the doors to the kennels, and loud barks make it hard to think. I smile. I love the sound of barking.

"The red dots mean they just got out of surgery and are on a twenty-four hour hold until they will be available for adoption. You can come back and meet with the dog. Green means the dog is good to go. Orange means special medical needs. Just grab one of us when you decide. We hope your fur-ever friend is here," he laughs at his own joke. "I love that one. It's great." He shakes his head at himself as he walks away, sighing from how hard he cracks himself up.

"No sissy dogs," Logan warns. "Ankle biters are evil fuckers. They can't protect you." Logan pushes me forward to the middle aisle, and there are kennels on either side of us. I want to take every single dog home.

Tears burn my eyes when I see some of the dogs laying on the floor curled in on themselves like they have given up. Some are barking and jumping, wanting out, needing human interaction. I bring my hand to my mouth to cover a sob, and Logan stops us when he notices that I'm not having a good time.

Nothing about this is good.

"Hey..." He brushes the tear off my cheek. "I know, little sparrow. I know." He pulls me against his rock-solid body, holding his hand on the back of my head to press it against his chest. I inhale the scent of leather and the familiar smell of pine, reminding me of the time I hiked through the forest.

"I want them all," I sniffle, and I doubt he can hear me since my lips are against his shirt, muffling my words.

"I'll figure out a way for you to have anything you want."

I'm not sure what that means since we don't know each other. I want to know him, more than I've ever wanted to know anyone in my life. He doesn't seem dangerous. He doesn't seem all that bad and scary like my father describes the Ruthless Kings.

"We can save two of them today. Let's do that." Logan pushes me away and presses a kind, comforting kiss on my forehead.

We walk up and down the plain cement floors, staring into each cage that holds a cute, precious life. I stop at one that is just sitting there, staring at us with a tilt of his head. The dog is pure black, a German Shepard mix with bright blue eyes. He is gorgeous. What is with the color black coming into my life lately?

"Hi, there—" I peek at the nametag on the silver gate. "Tyrant. Oh, is that what you are?" I talk to him, hoping he understands me. He puts one paw in front of the other to sniff my hand that is stretched for him. He peers up at me with those see-through eyes, trying to get a feel for who I am. His cold black nose hits my palm, and I giggle when he licks me next.

"He's beautiful," Logan says, squatting at the next cage over. "And so are you, beautiful." The dog barks, not liking the compliment. "Oh, my mistake. You are a handsome man, Yeti." The name makes sense since the dog is pure white.

"I think we found our dogs," I say, scratching behind Tyrant's ear.

"Let me go wave the guy down. Can I say that I'm glad you didn't get a small dog?"

"Well, I want to be protected. I do live alone," I say.

"No husband or boyfriend?" he fishes, eyeing me from the side while he pets Yeti.

"Um, no. Not even a contender."

"I think you have one."

I turn my head to the left to see if he's joking, but his faces is serious, and his inky black eyes stare at me with so much intensity that I have to glance away. I clear my throat and stand, waving my hand in the air to gain the attention of one of the volunteers so I can meet Tyrant. Logan is too much for me right now; too much man, too much of everything I've ever dreamed of. Having him say things like that when my father hates him and the club, it doesn't make our future hold any promise.

It makes it long, bumpy, and ending with a bad collision. I'll have my heart broken, a ruined relationship with my father, and Logan will probably be on to the next innocent, little virgin girl. Or not. Maybe guys like him like sluts. Nothing wrong with that life, women power, and all that; it just isn't my thing.

It's better to get away from Logan now because the disaster he will leave my heart in when he's done running it over with his motorcycle will be impossible to clean up.

I don't look back at Logan when the volunteer takes Tyrant from his cage and to a private room where he and I can meet. I try not to think about the kiss in the rain, another miracle that will be less likely to happen again—like the rain.

I toss the ball against the wall, and Tyrant runs to get it, brings it to me, drops it, and sits proud and regal. He's trained. Who on earth would surrender this dog to a shelter?

"You're a good boy, aren't you?" I baby talk to him, rubbing his sides until his tail thuds on the ground. "You want to come home with me?"

Tyrant barks and licks the sides of my face.

"I'll take that as a yes." I wipe my cheek on my shoulder, the wet slobber thick.

"How is it going in here?"

I glance up at the associate and nod. "Sign me up. We are going home," I tell him, and he leads me out front with a new red collar and matching leash. I pay the fee, and ten minutes later I'm walking out with a new friend.

Only to be stopped by one I never should have made.

"Leaving without telling me goodbye, little sparrow?" Logan leans against the wall, and a muscular white Pitbull sits between his feet looking just as lethal and powerful as his new owner.

I'm not going to ask where the nickname came from because I'm already attached. I need to pull away before I find myself stupid in love with a troublemaker. "You know this can't happen, Logan," I tell him softly, barely able to meet his eyes. They make it difficult to verbalize words when they hypnotize me into a dazed state. "We are attracted to each other, but that's all it is. This will never work. The MC you're with, my father wants to take you down. It's his mission—"

"Do you even want to know why? Or are you just wanting to paint me and my club brothers with the same brush? Judging us before you get to know us? I'll admit, I haven't done great things in my past, but I'm opening a business. I don't deal dope or whatever the fuck you think I do."

"I—" I snap my jaw shut when I realize I don't have anything to say. If I want to be honest with myself, that's exactly what I thought they did. Drugs, weapons, murder, all the stuff that people fear.

"Wow." He chuckles, but it has a disappointing beat that chastises me, bringing guilt on my shoulders. "I thought you were different from the rest of the women, but you're just another bitch, aren't you?"

I don't even think. I rear my hand back, clench my fist, and punch Logan right in the face. He barely moves, and his skin only reddens from the small hit. I never said I was a pro. Tyrant growls, and Yeti does the same. They face up just like Logan and I are.

The four us are showing teeth and ready to attack. "You listen to me, Logan. I'm naïve about a lot of things, but one thing I do know is I'm not like the women in your life, so you don't get to call me a bitch. I won't stand for it. You proved to me just then why I should have nothing to do with you. Even if you aren't breaking the law, why would I want to be with a man who looks at women as bitches? If anyone is the bitch here, princess," I spit the first nickname he gave me, "it's you." I push a finger into his chest, trying not to think about how firm it is with muscle.

"Let's go, Tyrant." I march my way toward my car and begin to panic because I just punched the Vice President, which sounds pretty important, of a motorcycle club. What if he calls a hit out on my head? And then I'm taken to a dark room where they will tie me up and—crap—I pinch my eyes shut when my nightmare suddenly turns into a sexual fantasy with Logan tying me to a bedpost. "No, that's not what would happen, and you know it,

Juliette." I press the button on my key ring to open my doors, let Tyrant in the back, and then sit in the driver's seat.

I take a few breaths, calming my racing heart. My knuckles are red, and they're starting to throb from hitting his cheek. Is he made of steel? It's unfair that his body is molded from stone. My fist never stood a chance.

"What did I do?" I look in the rearview to see him letting Yeti into the truck. He must feel eyes on him because he looks directly at me and then blows me a kiss.

Blows me a freaking kiss! After I punched him.

He is certifiable. What guy wants anything to do with a girl after that? I don't regret it. No one calls me a bitch and gets away with it.

I also owe him an apology for judging him, but I think we need to let bygones be bygones and go our separate ways.

If I know that, then why do I think about his kiss for the rest of night?

I'm lying in bed, Yeti on the other side of me taking up the majority of the mattress. He's on his back, jowls flopped back to expose his teeth while loud snores come from him. I'm glad he can sleep because I've tossed and turned all night thinking about that tiny little fist connecting with my cheek. It didn't hurt at all, but it was hot.

She is so feisty and strong, and I love how she stands up for herself. I shouldn't have called her a bitch, but those feelings of hatred overcoming love came forward, and it seemed like she hated 'my kind' of people.

What I didn't think about in that moment, like I'm thinking right now, is that she doesn't understand people like me. She doesn't know enough.

"Tool!" Reaper's loud voice shakes my closed door. "Get out here! Now!"

Shit. I hate that tone. This can't be good. "Coming!" I roll out of bed, slide on my pants, shirt, cut, and boots, and Yeti doesn't even move. "Yeti, get your ass out of bed. Let's go."

He grumbles, clearly not happy with getting out of bed, and snorts.

"You and me both. Let's go." Yeti follows behind me, his nails clicking against the hardwood floor as I hoof it down the hallway to the main room. Church is always in the chapel, but every member is gathered in a circle, looking down at the ground. "What's going on?" I ask, stepping through Skirt and Poodle to get a view of what has captured everyone's attention. When I get to the forefront of the group, what I see makes my blood run cold. "What the fuck?" I say with disbelief as I stare at one of our dead members.

Ghost.

We haven't seen him in a while. He decided to go nomad about a year ago. He travels a lot, and if he needs a place to stay, he goes to another chapter.

He's bound, gagged, and there's a screwdriver between his eyes.

My signature.

"I have a feeling this is for you, Tool," Reaper points out the obvious.

"Yeah, I'd fucking say so," I squat and turn Ghost onto his back. His lips are stitched shut, I notice; something that isn't part of my signature. "How did they get ahold of him? Reaper, whoever did this knows that I kill with a screwdriver. That means it's member. We have a snitch."

"Think that's why his lips are stitched closed?" Badge steps forward, his eyes analyzing the body like he would at a crime scene. "Maybe it's symbolic."

"What do you mean?" I'm doing my best to think like Badge, the cop, but my abilities are pretty limited. Cars, bikes, blood. That's about all I'm good for.

Badge mirrors my position, bending his knees to get a closer look at Ghost. The poor bastard. Looks like he went through a lot of pain before death finally knocked on his door. Badge reaches into his cut pocket and pulls out one of his riding gloves and slips it on his hand. He lifts the ropes on Ghost's wrists, seeing red marks and deep cuts, then checks the wound site around Ghost's lips.

"Ghost was alive when his lips were sealed shut, I'm guessing. See the red areas and how tight the thread is? Ghost fought. The deep cuts around his wrists says he has been in those ropes for a few days, and when the person didn't get what he wanted out of Ghost, he made sure Ghost could never speak again."

"That's sick," I tell him.

"You should cut the stiches and open his mouth." Tongue takes out his blade, and the steel rings when he flips it open. He kneels on the floor on the other side of Ghost, placing the sharp metal against Ghost's lips.

I snatch his wrist, stopping him from defiling one of our brothers. "Let him rest in peace, Tongue. Right now isn't the time for you to get your rocks off on someone's mouth."

Tongue rips his arm away from my hold and sneers. "I'm not doing it to get my dick hard. The mouth, the tongue, it's what tells truths or lies."

"Yeah, that's why his mouth is stitched shut," I say with a hard edge to my voice. I'm not in the mood for Tongue's weird shit.

"No, Tongue is on to something. A lot of the times, in crime scenes that I've seen, the killer will leave a note in the person's mouth. Do it, Tongue," Badge says.

I glance up at Reaper, stunned that he's going to let this happen. "Reaper? Come on, man. Ghost has been through enough."

"Let them do what they need to do," Reaper ignores my plea, and Tongue cuts each string in quick jerks until the lips are free.

"Rigor is setting in. I'll need help opening his jaw." Badge looks up at me and then Tongue, wondering which one of us will help him.

Tongue grasps the lower jaw, and Badge starts to part Ghost's lips. "Shit," Badge says when we see that all of Ghost's teeth have been taken out.

I look away, hating that he went through so much torture only to end up dead. Usually that's how torture works, though. You never keep a loose end alive, but I never expected Ghost to get clipped.

"Look at that. Tongue's right." Badge reaches into Ghost's mouth and pulls out a bloody piece of paper.

"The tongue is still intact, so they easily could have taken that to keep him silent too."

Both Badge and I give Tongue a look that tells him to shut up and be quiet. At this point, how Ghost is silent doesn't really matter.

"What? It's an observation," he mumbles.

"You're a fucking weirdo," Badge tells Tongue as he unfolds the small piece of paper that was lodged in our club brother's mouth.

I try to figure out what Badge is thinking as he reads the note. His eyes move, but his face gives nothing away. He purses his lips together and holds up the note for Prez to take. Reaper exhales as he reaches out and takes the paper.

Reaper never hides how pissed off he is, and right now, if it was possible, steam would be pouring from his nose like an angry bull ready to charge and spear someone through the heart with his horn. "Looks like we have a new threat, boy," he says, passing me the note.

I read the note out loud, thinking everyone deserves to know and be on their toes anytime they go out.

"And one by one the Kings fall along with their empire."

"What's that mean?" Poodle asks.

"Means whoever is doing this isn't going to stop until every single one of us are dead," Badge says and stands, turning his neck side to side to crack it.

The entire clubhouse goes up in a roar, nothing can be

understood. Everyone is yelling and panic is setting in. Reaper places his fingers in his mouth and blows, a high-pitched whistle pierced through the air, and everyone immediately shuts up. Even Yeti falls to his stomach and lands his eyes on Reaper, the man in charge.

"Bitching and yelling about it isn't going to get anything done!" he bellows, and Sarah takes a hold of his hand, laying her head on his shoulder. Reaper closes his eyes, takes a deep breath, and calms. "Being at each other's throats will only make matters worse. From here on out, everyone will be in pairs. No one, I repeat, no one is to walk alone. If I find out that someone walked alone, there will be punishment. I don't want to see this happen to another one of my members."

"How did he get here?" I ask, wondering how they got inside the gate without anyone knowing.

"Whoever did this dumped him at the start of the driveway. I saw him when I pulled in," Badge says right before his cell phone rings. "I got to take this. It's the department." He steps over Ghost, and a few members part for him to get by, and he disappears in the kitchen.

"Let's bury him in the plot." Reaper rubs his eyes, and he looks like he's about to pass the gavel down from being tired of dealing with the shit that falls at our doorstep.

The plot is the MC cemetery that's located at the back of the property. It's where all the members who have died are buried.

"I think this has something to do with the sheriff." I stand in front of Reaper, and Sarah stands up and gives him a kiss on the cheek before heading to the room they keep at the clubhouse. "It makes sense. He is in law enforcement. Badge works for him, and that makes Badge a target since he works in close proximity."

"Sheriff hates us, sure, but what good does he get out of doing this?"

"It takes us out as a threat."

"How would he know of Ghost? Of how you…" Reaper looks left and right to make sure no one is around. "Of how you kill. None of it makes sense."

"I'm assuming he has files on all of us. Most of us have been arrested, Reaper. We're in the system. As of how he knows about me, I don't know. No one knows about that…" I think about what happened all those years ago.

"What?" Reaper grips me by the shoulders and shakes me. "Spit it out, Tool."

"You know the story of when I was fifteen…" I close my eyes and wonder if somehow, in some way, what I did all those years ago is coming to haunt me. It's haunted me enough in my dreams, but now it has to fuck me up in real life.

"What about it?"

"Well, it was my mom." I move out of the way when Bullseye and Doc pick up Ghost's body.

"I'm going to embalm him and clean him up. He deserves that," Doc says, lifting Ghost's heavy legs as Bullseye lifts the torso. Bullseye winces and already starts to sweat from the pain in his chest.

Reaper gives him a tilt of a chin as Doc and Bullseye carry Ghost out of the room

"Reaper, it was me and my mom there, but there's the Boston Ruthless chapter too. They knew I killed my father."

"Brass wouldn't rat you out, and neither would Knox. Doesn't explain how the sheriff would know." Reaper stares up at the ceiling, and his pulse jumps in his neck. "I don't feel like dealing with this right now. Follow the sheriff, find out what information you can. I don't care what you have to do. I want answers. I'll talk to Badge too. We need information. We need to figure out what the hell is going on and why the world seems to want us burnt to the damn ground." He turns on his boot and lumbers to the room Sarah is in. No doubt about to have an angry fuck; that's what I would do if I had a woman.

Which reminds me of Juliette and Reaper's warning. The one way to get close to the sheriff is to get close to his daughter. I'll be doing the club a favor by getting to know her. Going against the Prez's orders for the good of the club, sometimes that's what needs to be done.

I have a feeling Juliette Johnson is about to give me the fight of my life, and I'm not going to resist at all. I want to know what it's like to feel something other than hate again, and Juliette is the answer to that.

I just hope she can get past her father's hate for me.

Because when hate clashes against hate, there's only one

outcome.

Destruction.

"What am I doing? What am I doing? Nothing. I'm doing nothing. I'm getting my oil changed. Cars need their oil changed. It's normal," I talk to myself as I drive down the road to Kings' Garage, that's on Ruthless King's property. My car doesn't need an oil change, but I want to see Logan. I want to be able to determine for myself what he's like.

My dad has controlled me and the decisions I've made long enough. I want to think for myself and see if Logan is the man my dad makes him out to be.

A lawbreaking criminal.

"What do you think, Tyrant? Am I crazy?" I glance over to the passenger seat and see him curled up in a ball, his bushy tail covering his nose as he naps. "You're not much help." I drive away from the main strip and out toward the desert. There isn't a lot of traffic on the lonely road. It's just sand on either side of me for miles.

Until a large fortress comes to view. Everyone knows who lives here. The land is different than what it looked like a few months ago. Now, there's a large iron gate that seals their property. It gives me the impression that anyone who gets uninvited won't get out. I turn on my blinker and take a left and follow the dirt road for a minute or so before I come to the gate where someone is on watch.

The man is big, or maybe he just looks big because he's dressed in all black and has tattoos everywhere. He knocks on my window, and I do the smart thing and press the button to roll it down. And since I'm so smart, I don't roll it all the way down, just halfway.

"State your business." His breath reeks of rum. I can't believe he's upright. My eyes glance to the name on his cut, and it says Pirate. "Girl, did you hear me? State your damn business," he snaps at me, and it makes me jump in my seat.

Tyrant wakes up and sits on his haunches, growling at the man who's giving me demands.

"I'm here to get my oil changed—"

"We aren't doing oil changes today. Business is closed."

"I—" Crap. What am I going to do? I need to see Logan. "Is Tool around? I really need to speak with him."

"I knew a girl like you wouldn't come poking around in a place like this. Tell me, what do you want with Tool that I can't help you out with, sweet thing?" Pirate leans his arms against the car and licks his lips, looking my body up and down. "Bet you're better than any club whore. Tool really has outdone himself with you."

"This was a mistake; I need to go." I place the car in reverse, but Pirate snakes one arm through the window.

"Where you going, baby? I can make you feel just as good as he can." Pirate tries to take the wheel from me, but I act fast and slam on the gas. The tires spin against the red sand, sending a cloud of dust up in the air and encompassing us in a small cloud. Finally, the tires get traction, and the car speeds away.

Tears burn my eyes from fear, and I do my best to control the steering wheel as Pirate runs by the side of the car and keeps his hand on the wheel. The car swings left and right as we battle for control. I press the gas harder, and Pirate loses his grip when he can't keep up with me. He falls flat on his face in the dirt. I don't look back. I keep my eyes focused, watching where I'm going and jerk the wheel to the right. I slam on the brake when I get on the road.

The smell of burning rubber invades my air vents. My throat is dry from breathing so fast. I need to get the hell out of here. I put the car in drive, press the gas, and peel out of there like a bat out of hell.

What was I thinking? I can't believe I thought getting in there to see Tool would be easy. It's best to just forget about him. We don't mesh. Our lives are too different, and nothing but trouble can come from them.

A low grumble vibrates the floor of my car. I look in the rearview mirror and see a bike is following me. "Oh crap," I squeak and press on the gas more, watching the needle on the speedometer climb higher the faster I go. The bike is catching up quick, and the round headlight reflects off the sun and blinds me for a moment.

Holy crap, I'm trying to get away from a biker. This is a high-speed chase! I'm scared. It's thrilling, and I kind of never want it to end, but I know whatever that biker has in store for me can't be good. I bypass the strip to get to my house. I can get there, lock the door, and everything will be fine.

Tyrant barks, and I pet his neck, doing my best to be reassuring. "I know. We're going to be okay. I'm going to get us home." And then I don't know what will happen, but at least I'll be safe in the comfort of my own house. Maybe. If the biker wants to, he can get in by breaking a window or the door.

I really haven't thought this through, but I have no choice at this point. Home is closer than the police department. Sweat is sliding down the back of my neck from my hairline, and when I take the turn to get to my house, I take an immediate left down another road, then a right, before getting back onto the main road. I don't see or hear a bike now.

"I think we're safe, Tyrant," I whisper and pat his head, but he ducks his snout, growling. He doesn't believe me, but I'm not going to put us in any more danger. Nope. I learned my lesson. No more visiting biker clubhouses. Dad is officially right. They are trouble.

My house finally comes to view, and I pull into the driveway and waste no time getting out of the car. "Come, Tyrant. Come on." I clap my hand against my thigh, and Tyrant jumps from the passenger seat across the driver's and onto the gravel. My spine tingles, the hair on the back of my neck stands up, and as I look around, taking in my surroundings, I don't see anything off-putting.

"Let's go inside, boy." I open the gate to the front lawn and bounce up the steps.

Sliding the key into the lock, I turn it and open the front door, hanging my keys on a notch I nailed to the wall on the right. Tyrant growls and barks, his saliva dripping as he stares down the hallway. The hair on his back is standing up, telling me that something is very wrong. I open my purse and grab the gun my dad makes me carry. I always thought my dad was crazy for suggesting this weapon, but now that I'm in my house and my dog is going nuts, I'm going to have to send Dad a thank you card.

I click the safety off and somehow keep my gun up in the air while my arms shake. The only room down this hall is the guest bathroom and a closet, and no one can fit in that closet. It's a shoebox. My right hand stays on the gun while I push the bathroom door open with my left. I flip on the light and notice nothing out of the norm.

Tyrant runs in the bedroom and starts barking again, and I follow after him, afraid that he will get hurt without me there.

"Tyrant!" I scream and point my gun left to right to see Tyrant on the bed, sitting next to Logan. He looks calm and collected, petting Tyrant with a smirk on his lips.

"Hey, little sparrow, mind putting that gun down?" he says in a voice that is deep and sexy, causing a gush to flood my panties, and my slit aches for his touch.

I slide the safety on and set the gun on top of my armoire. "Logan," I breathe, placing my palm to my chest as my heart thumps wildly. I don't know why I think my hand will make my heart slow down because it never does. "What are you doing here?" I question and do my best not to think about how good he looks in my bed. He looks different today, tired with dark circles under his eyes and a sadness I can't explain, but it's there. I walk to the end of my bed and slide my eyes over his long legs.

They are like tree trunks, thick with muscle that I want to climb until I'm settled in the middle of his lap.

Oh, this is bad. A Ruthless King member is in my bed, and I want him to stay there and let me see how ruthless he can be.

"Pirate said you wanted to see me, Juliette."

My eyes bug out and nearly fall to the floor. "That was you on the bike? I thought I lost you. How did you know I lived here?"

Logan's large hand strokes Tyrant's head, and he lays down, the traitor, and closes his eyes, enjoying the biker's touch. I just bet he is!

I scoff internally; am I really mad at a dog about getting the attention I want?

Yes, I'm that petty apparently.

"You might want to take your last name off your mailbox if you don't want anyone to know where you live. Now tell me, why did you come see me?"

Drat. "I came to get my oil changed, but Pirate scared me off. He came on really strong, and it scared me."

Logan leans forward from relaxing against the headboard. "Did he touch you? Pirate is a drunk asshole and usually harmless, but did he touch you?" The way his black brows flex and furrow makes it look like a storm cloud has covered his face, darkening it with a menacing tendency.

"No, I mean, he implied that he wanted to. He said he can give me what you can, and I didn't like that, so I sped out of there." I look away, ashamed that I left in such a hurry, scared like a little girl. I can't handle one drunk guy. No wonder my dad was afraid for me to be out on my own.

"I'll kill him," he growls, and the low vibration rattling his chest has my nipples tenting my dress. "Fucker better drink his last bottle of rum because it will be farewell and good riddance." He's seething with rage, but I don't know why he cares about a man wanting me. He doesn't want me, right?

I lay my hand on his ankle and lift my eyes to his, looking at him through my lashes. "It's okay. Don't worry about it. I shouldn't have gone there anyway. I was in over my head."

"A girl like you needing an oil change can go anywhere; why come to me? I'm sure your dad knows how to change oil in a car."

I hate my pale skin. My blood rushes to my cheeks and burns, and I know he can see how red my face is.

"You want to see me," he says when he figures it out. "Even though you punched me, you still like me."

I push a piece of hair behind my ear and hold my chin high. "I don't know what you mean. I don't know you enough to like you. And I shouldn't. Since women are bitches."

"You judged me, but I should have been better and not called you that. It wasn't right of me, and I'm sorry."

The last thing I expect is for him to apologize for anything. He doesn't seem like the type who admits when he's wrong too often. It's only fair that I push pride away and apologize for punching him, even though I can see it barely left a mark. "I'm sorry too."

"Good, so we can start over?" Logan swings his long legs around to the edge of the bed and stands to his intimidating height. In two long strides he's in front of me, holding out his hand. "I'm Logan, and everyone calls me Tool because of this." He points to the screwdriver above his ear.

"I'm Juliette, and I'm not everyone. I'm going to call you Logan." I slide my hand into his and he squeezes it firmly, rubbing his thumb along mine.

He hums, amused by my answer, and in a move I'm not expecting, he tugs me closer to his body. A quick inhale and leather invades my senses as his beard brushes the top of my forehead, and I close my eyes, enjoying the small touch. I don't know how to do this, to be with a man, and with how he handles me, I don't know if he knows how to be with me either.

"I'm going to say one thing and one thing only before I kiss you and strip you naked, Juliette," Logan warns, brushing his lips over my cheek. My entire body feels the slight brush of the mouth I've gotten myself off to. My breath hitches, and I wait for him to finish what he's going to say as his hands cup my face. The callouses scratch the surface of my skin, and my lips part from how good it feels. "I don't know how to feel for anything that's good for me," he admits, sliding his lips down the sensitive flesh below my ear.

"Maybe I'm not good for you," I counter as my head lulls back on my shoulders, giving him access to my neck.

"Oh, I know you aren't." His voice deepens, and one of his hands wraps around my neck. "You're going to get me killed, and while the outcome is bad, I have a feeling the journey is going to feel good."

I don't know what he means when he says I can get him killed, but I'm not able to think of that for much longer when his lips land on mine. My ability to process any thought fly out the window. The hairs on his beard scratch my upper lip when he changes the angle of his head and pulls me tighter to his body.

His lips promise something dangerous as they take my mouth in a possessive drive. His tongue dances against mine, twirling and dipping inside my mouth with expertise. He groans down my throat, and I reply in a quiet whimper, fisting his shirt in my hands. Logan presses his hips against mine, and that's when I feel his hard cock pressing against my thigh.

He is huge. Everything I knew he would be. It only makes sense, since the rest of him is so big.

My lips are numb and tingling when he pulls away and lays his forehead on mine. "You feel..." He says it in a way like he can't believe his own feelings.

"Good," I finish for him. "You feel good." I swallow to dislodge the lump in my throat. This isn't a good idea. There isn't a future here, but I think we both know that.

"Yeah." He nods. "Good."

The word is spoken with such uncertainty and a little distaste. I can't figure out if that means he likes it or not.

I'm about to pull away when he grabs the back of my head and smashes his lips against mine. It's forceful this time, aggressive, like he's getting to taste something he will never get to have again. He pushes me down on the bed, causing Tyrant to jump off. I look up at him in a glossy daze, enjoying the arousal through my body.

There's no one here to stop us or interrupt, which has me wondering if this will end sooner rather than later because my dad always has someone come by every day. He shrugs off his leather cut and then, in a sexy move, he reaches behind his head and grabs the collar of his shirt and pulls it off.

Showing lines of hard muscle and tattoos. Logan's body is the most of a man I have ever seen, and I have a feeling he's more man than the ones I've ever met.

9
TOOL

What the hell am I doing putting my dirty hands all over this beautiful sparrow? I'm insane. I'm out of my mind, but I have to admit, it feels so… I hate to say the word, but I feel fucking good. I know it will all come crashing down because that's life; that's what happens when things are good. They go bad in a blink of a damn eye.

And it's only a matter of time before she hates me too. I came here looking for … I don't know what. After Pirate told me she was at the clubhouse looking for me, after I just got done burying one of my brothers, being around her sounded all too good.

Now I'm here, and she makes the bad inside me bury itself instead of letting it stay on the surface. She pulls the good out of me, and I want to be that for her, I do, but I'm far from it.

I've killed.

I've tortured.

I've enjoyed some of it, most of it, but how can hands like mine appreciate something so beautiful, when all they have done is seen evil?

"You're gorgeous," she says whispers as she trails her hands from my neck, down the middle of my chest and stomach. She isn't rushed while appreciating me.

I snag my hand around her wrist, stopping her from touching me like she's never touched a man before. I don't want to be appreciated. I don't deserve it.

"What is it?" she asks in a smooth rasp that has my cock pressing against my zipper. "Did I do something wrong?"

"No." I shake my head. How can I say that no one has ever touched me like that before? All the women I've been with have always been a quick fuck, in and out, that's it. No one has ever touched me with delicacy like that, like if she presses too hard, I'll break. I fall forward and catch myself on my hands as I cage her in, hovering over her succulent body. She licks her lips, plump and natural, not full of fake injections like a lot of women. They're so soft, and a small dimple creases her bottom lip from the flesh being so big.

I suck it into my mouth, nibble on it, and let it go with a pop. She moans and it's harmonic, like a damn song, and I'm drawn in. She's a siren, singing to lure her victims in before she makes the kill.

Her hands might not be the death of me, but somehow she'll still be the cause of it.

Taking her mouth again, I lower my body onto hers and let my hands fall between her knees and lift her dress slowly. I tear my lips away from hers, not wanting to miss the first time I get to see her body. The pink dress has her skin looking flawless, like glass, as if maybe she's the delicate one.

Slowly, her thighs come to view, and my hands grip the flesh. I can't stop the groan that takes over. I'm consumed by her body. Every fucking inch of her. She has to be made for me and my touch because there's no way a woman who looks like this doesn't exist for me and only me.

Her blue panties come to view, and a wet spot dampens in the gusset of them. The outline of her folds stick to the material, and my thumbs dive under the band near her groin. I bite my lip as I watch her writhe under me, a bright blush taking over her face while her hands grip the sheets.

So responsive.

My thumbs tease her lips, spreading them apart, and I hear the slurp of her juices sticking to her folds. I want down there. I want to taste her and ruin her for anyone else. She'll be mine, even if it means ruining her good and bringing her down to my filthy level.

She's soaked for me.

For. Me.

As much as I hate to, I leave her sweet cunt and lift her dress more. Her torso is next, and her waist is so small, a perfect dip where my hands belong, and that's exactly where they go. A rumble grows in my chest as I grip her ribcage, imagining how it will feel when I'm fucking her and holding on to her like this.

My hands wander up the swell of her tits, and her back arches off the bed when I tug the dress over them, seeing the silk of her bra.

"Fuck me," I say in appreciation, gripping the flesh firmly in my palms. So much of her tits spill from my fingers. So damn big. More for me to adore and lavish with my mouth. I can't wait to mark them with little love bites.

"I've always been fuller," she says and tries to cover herself with her arms, and I grab them, pinning her limbs to her sides.

"You won't deny me, little sparrow. You're fucking beautiful, and I want to see every fucking inch of you. I want to memorize every curve, every ridge, and I can't wait to have my mouth full of your tits. You're perfect." I pull the dress the rest of the way off, and her face is hidden for a second.

"Logan?" She says my name with a bit of hesitancy. "I need to tell you something."

"What is it?" I kiss the curve of her left breast, moaning from how soft her skin is, and continue to adore the other side with the same attention. She smells so good, like that fucking mango scent that I love so much. I want to eat her like the fruit too, only I'll never have to stop because this is never-ending helping of something delicious.

"I've never—"

The two words have my heart jackhammering when I lift

my gaze from her tits to her face. She's worrying her bottom lip between her teeth, and her face is as red as a tomato. She won't look at me. "It isn't because I don't want to or because I've waited for a reason. I haven't. My dad was too controlling—"

"Juliette." I grip her chin and pull myself up until my face is hovering over hers. "Don't talk about your dad when my cock is pressed against your thigh and mouth has kissed your tits."

"Right." She nods. "Right. Duh." She pretends to smack herself in the head, but it's harder than she intends, and she winces. "Ow, okay, I swear, I'm not a complete mess."

"Juliette, tell me." I know the words she's about to say, and I'm nervous, but I'm thrilled, but I'm a bastard who doesn't deserve her.

"I've never done any of this! I'm a virgin, but I don't want to be, so let's get on with it, okay? Come on." She claws at my back to hurry things along, and it makes me smile; she's nervous.

And she's crazy if she thinks I want to get this over with or rush it. One thing is for certain, I'm not fucking her today. I'm not ready for that, and I don't want to be the man she hates after she realizes I'm not good enough for her. I won't be the guy who takes her virginity and then have her regret it.

I don't want to be anyone's regret. I've lived that already.

"Juliette, calm down." I meet her eyes and can see that she's panicking and afraid, but not of what's happening between us, but because I might not want her now. "I love that," I tell her and kiss her deeply, showing just how much I love that I'm her first and wish we could take it further than it's about to go. "Relax, little sparrow. Let me make you feel good." I kiss her lips once more and work my way down her neck, nipping the middle of her throat.

I reach behind her and unsnap her bra, tossing the damn contraption aside to revel large, round, perky breasts. I whimper in adoration as I knead them, loving the weight and feel of them in my palms. There's nothing like a set of heavy breasts in a man's hand. She wiggles against me, her pelvis rocking against my cock. The move makes a flood of pre-come leave my slit, and I grunt, gripping her hip with my hand to stop her movement.

I'm about to fucking come in my jeans, and I can't let her see that she can get me off that fast. It isn't good for a man to be able to come so fast. Usually I don't because cut-sluts are easy, another hole just to fill the time, but Juliette isn't like that; she's different.

She's the good I need.

And I can't have.

I suck one nipple into my mouth, humming around the elongated bud and then bite down hard, causing her to cry out. Her hands grip the back of my head while digging her nails into my scalp. I've always been a man who loves a little pain with his pleasure. With a reluctant plop, I let go of the sweet morsel and lick down the middle of her body, dipping my tongue into her naval.

It's when I get to her panties that she's rubbing her thighs together and trying to push my head between her legs. I chuckle from her impatience and grab the thin panties and pull them free with a slight tug. They rip easily, and since I'm a collector of souvenirs, there's nothing better to remember our time together than to keep them. I stuff them in my jeans pocket and push her legs apart until her pink center is winking at me.

She's bare. All clean with no hair, and my cock grows harder. I rock against the mattress in dying fucking need of friction. "Such a pretty pussy, little sparrow. You're such a good girl keeping it for me." I blow cold air against her folds, and she shifts onto her elbows to get a better look at me.

"Logan—" she stutters when my tongue makes the first lick from the bottom of her cunt to the top, swirling the tip around her clit before sucking the bundle of nerves into my mouth. "Oh, god! Logan. Yes!" she moans, falling back onto the bed as I tongue fuck her. Her legs shake, and sweet cream sticks to my chin as the slick juices leave her virgin hole. My finger finds the untouched part of her and slides in, and the feel of her hot channel grasping me has my eyes rolling to the back of my head. She's so tight, I can't even fit another finger inside. I curl my digit up in a come-hither motion, pressing against a spot that will heighten her pleasure.

"What is that? Oh, fuck, so much better than any toy, Logan. Oh, yes!" She pinches her nipples and tugs, but my brows shoot to my hairline when I think of her playing with toys. I wonder what she has and if she'll let me use them on her.

Her legs tense around my neck, squeezing me until I can't breathe, but I don't take my face away from her cunt; not when she's so close. I can smell her orgasm from the nectar soaking my palm and the sheet beneath us.

I fuck her mouth the same way I fuck the bed now, hard and fast, needing her to get off, needing to get me off. Her taste is so good, I'm going to fucking come from it. There's no stopping it. She tastes like the one thing I've been afraid of my entire life. And it's so good, so right, so damn addicting that my heart is filling with hope.

I hate hope.

I hate good.

Hate is constant. Hate is natural. Hate is survival.

Not with her. Oh, it isn't with her.

It's opposite, and it's overwhelming my body, my system, and rewiring everything I feel and believe.

She's the refuge I've always wanted and never thought I'd have.

I pick her up by her thighs and dig my hands into her ass as I hold her in the air and feast on her sweet honeypot.

"Logan, Logan, Logan!" she chants as she falls apart in my arms and in my mouth, flooding my tongue with her sweet, savory sauce that I never want to leave my lips.

It's the first time a woman calls me by my real name in bed, and it sends me over the edge, filling my jeans with sticky cum, and I don't regret a thing. I groan into her pussy with pleasure and relief, never wanting this moment to end.

But like all good things…

I woke up alone this morning with not so much as a note from Logan, only his scent. It ticks me off and saddens me at the same time that he left without word. He's proving to be everything my father warned me about, and yet, I want more from Logan. Like an idiot.

I'm at work now, staring out the window of the lingerie store to see him and a few other of his club members working on the space he just bought. He hasn't looked over at me once. Why? We didn't have sex. It isn't like he got what he wanted and left. If anything, I'm the one who ended up getting all the pleasure.

Every now and then, when my hair moves over my shoulders or drops in my face, the scent of pine and leather fills my nose. It hits my stomach like a deadweight or wrecking ball, reminding me of the best night I've ever had in my entire life only to be left feeling used.

I glance out the window again, hanging a black lingerie set on the gold rack and miss the notch. It falls to the floor, and I bend down and stay there for a minute to get my head together. I need to get him out of my head.

The image of his mouth sucking my clit comes to the forefront of my mind, and it takes my breath away. No man has ignited pleasure so quickly on my body like Logan has. One touch, a simple finger against a small part of my pleasure, and he sparks a raging wildfire, and the only way it can be tamed is if he puts it out himself.

"Are you going to stay down there all day? Do you want water? A drink? A pillow?" Trixie, the manager and my friend, teases me when she sits crossed legged next to me. "I see the appeal. It's a bit cooler down here and darker since the sun is coming through the windows. You know, I still think I need to get them tinted." She clicks her tongue then nods as if it's the greatest idea she has ever thought of. "I think I'll do that." She claps her hands, and her long nails that are always painted a bright color—today they are neon pink—click together.

"What's on your mind, Juliette?" she asks, lifting a tattooed brow at me. She's a bit older, in her forties I think, but she acts like she's twenty. The woman is young at heart, and she lets it show. It's what I love so much about her.

I pick up the lingerie set and stand, putting it on the hanger and shrug. "I don't know what you're talking about."

"Mmmhmm, you can't get nothing by me, girly. You're

sulking."

"Am not," I gasp.

"Are too."

"Am not!" I defend myself and then laugh at how childish we sound. I roll my eyes and give in. "Fine. I'm sulking. Happy?" I take another set of lingerie out of the cardboard box, this one is pink with little ribbons lacing up the sides. It's so cute, but no way will my boobs fit in this tiny thing. I grab a gold hanger and slide the straps through and make sure it looks pristine before setting it on the rack.

"Happy, girly," Trixie tsks and spins me around by digging her talons in my arm. Those suckers hurt. "I don't like to see you sulking; talk to me."

I let out a weighted sigh and look out the window again. "See the man with his shirt off?"

Trixie giggles. "Girly, they all have their shirts off, and I must say, it's a sight for sore eyes. My god."

"Oh, you're right. I didn't notice they were all shirtless." My eyes are zeroed in on Logan, and he still has that damn screwdriver over his ear. Why is he so attached to that thing? His tattoos shine in the sunlight, rolling with the flex of his muscles as he tosses chunks of wood in a dumpster. He's renovating the old Italian restaurant across the strip, and that means he's a handyman too. Perfect. He's perfect. I want to hate him.

"Which one are you looking at, girly?" Trixie asks and then claps her hands in front of her again when she gets an idea. "Oh, wait. Let me guess..." She points to all of them, humming as she thinks, and a smile takes over my face at her antics. She's crazy, but the good kind of crazy. "That one." She points to Logan, and my mouth drops open when she guesses right.

"How do you know that?" I'm baffled.

"Girly, I'm old not dead. Plus, I see how you look at him, and he looks at you."

"He doesn't look at me." I shake my head, not believing that for a second.

Her nails tap on the wall as she leans against it. Her eyes narrow at me as she thinks. Her hair is big and puffy from a perm that went bad a few weeks ago, but it looks good still, somehow. She can pull off anything with her personality. The crazy woman is wearing a jean mini skirt with purple leggings and a hot pink shirt that's a second skin, and the straps hug her shoulders. She looks like she has stepped out of the eighties every day, and I love every bit of it.

"Something happened between you and that tattooed meat stick," she guesses.

I snort and cover my mouth as a laughing fit takes over. "Meat stick?"

"Girly, meat stick. Meaning, everything about that man you want to eat up like a savage. So tell me, what happened?"

"Something that shouldn't have," I mutter and throw the lingerie in my hand down. "My dad warned me to stay away from him because he's part of the Ruthless Kings MC. We shared a night together—we didn't have sex—but I woke up alone without a word from him. I'm drawn to him, Trix. I can't explain it, and I don't want it to hurt that he decided to leave me alone, but it does."

"Why does your dad have a problem with the MC? They do so much good for this town. You know, I wouldn't have this shop if it wasn't for Reaper. I know him because of my brother, Hawk. He died a long time ago, and he was in the MC. Reaper made sure I was set up and taken care of. They do a lot of charity work. They are good men."

I had no idea. Dad only talks about them in a negative way. "I'm sorry about your brother," I say, placing a hand on her shoulder, and she taps my bicep.

"It's okay. I've learned to live without him for a while now. Listen, girly, coming from a woman who knows all about bikers, a lot of them aren't warm and fuzzy. A lot of them are dangerous, a lot of them have done things that would ruin people forever if they knew the truth. If he's all alpha and dominant, I'm sure he thinks the best thing for him to do is leave you alone. It's why my brother never really settled down. He had two kids with some club whores, on accident, and they turned out great. Reaper is married to Sarah, actually; my niece. I don't get to see her too much, though. I met her late in her life, so we don't really know each other."

"Maybe you should change that, Trixie," I offer her some advice too, and she smiles.

"Only if you go talk to that meat stick."

"Stop calling him that!" I flick her with the lace teddy.

"You know I'm right." Her eyes look through the window again and widen. "Oh, no." She points, and I follow her finger to see what has losing her humor.

My dad is out front of the old restaurant, and he's just handcuffed Logan. I run out the door and hurry across the street. A car slams on its brakes and almost hits me. My hands reach out and hit the hood. "I'm sorry," I mouth before taking off again, and my dad stops in his tracks because Logan is putting up a fight, trying to get his arms free as he looks at me.

"Dad, what are you doing?"

"This doesn't concern you, Juliette. Logan McGraw is being arrested for murder."

"That's ridiculous!" Logan defends himself and tries to pull free from my dad's hold again. "I haven't killed anyone. I've been here."

"Where were you last night?" my dad's question has my chest seizing up. Logan stares at me, jaw clenching, but he keeps his mouth shut. "That's what I thought."

"You have no proof. You just want to arrest me," Logan says, and one of his club brothers steps forward, wiping the sweat off his forehead with a shirt.

"We'll get you a lawyer, Tool. Don't worry. He has no evidence."

"I'll get my fucking evidence to take you bastards down!"

"Dad!" I can't believe what I'm hearing. This isn't the man who raised me. "You can't arrest him, and you know it. Let him go."

"Juliette, I'll tell you one more time—this has nothing to do with you."

"It's okay," Logan says to me. "I'll be fine."

"It isn't okay. He was with me last night, Dad. That's where he was. Let him go. He has an alibi."

"Oh shit," one of the MC members says.

"Fuck," another chimes in. "This just went from bad to worse."

"No daughter of mine would be caught dead with biker scum. You don't have to protect him, Juliette."

"I'm not, Dad. I'm telling you the truth. You're arresting the wrong man. He was with me all night."

I never seen my father so angry. He lifts his hand and before I have time to think, he backhands me across the face. I stumble back and hold my hand against my cheek. One of the guys catches me and turns me around to face him. "You okay?" he asks, trying to take my hand off my cheek, but I'm too stunned to move.

My father has never hit me before.

"What the fuck?" Logan snarls and gets free of my dad's hold. He spins around, and the man with a dart somehow uses it to unlock the cuffs. Logan runs to me, and I let him pull my hand off my face. He growls, gently brushing his knuckles over the red welted flesh. It burns. "You'd hit your own daughter!" Logan raises his voice at my dad, and I look to the left to see Trixie outside the store with her hand over her mouth.

"I'd hit my own daughter any time if it means she's turning into one of your fucking sluts," my dad spits, and the venom in his voice lands on me, and suddenly it's hard to breathe.

Logan pushes me behind him, and his arms flex. His body shakes, wanting to kill my father for what he's done, but that will only make matters worse. I rub my hand down his back, and he relaxes in an instant.

"Juliette, if you're with them, you're no daughter of mine," my father says before walking to his patrol car. He drives away, flipping the switch for the sirens, and I'm left wondering if my dad is the real monster in this scenario now.

"Are you okay?" Logan turns to me once my father is out of sight. "Let me see."

"I'm fine," I say in a distant voice. "I… I need to go back to work. I'll see you around."

"Juliette, no." Logan pulls me back to him, and his eyes dart over my face. He wants to say something, to say anything, but he doesn't. He presses his lips against my forehead and lets me go.

Without another word, I rub my cheek and walk across the street, wondering when my dad became so violent. Maybe the real enemy is the one I've been living with, not the one I've been warned about.

The only man I've wanted to kill more than my own father is Sheriff Johnson. After he hit Juliette, it took all I had not to snap his fucking neck. No one puts their hands on a woman, and no one puts their hands on my fucking woman.

If I kill him, I'll go to jail, and Juliette will hate me. Jail I can live with, but Juliette's hate is something I don't think I can.

I'm debating if the best thing she needs right now is me. If I stay away, her life will be better, but on the other hand, if I stay away, my life won't be.

"Do you think he saw us?" Knives, my ride along buddy for the night, asks. Him and Tongue are similar in a lot of ways. They have this obsession with blades, only Knives plays with the ninja stars, rolling them around on his finger. Sometimes, he accidently pricks himself from the sharp edges, and his knuckles are all scarred and fucked up from the metal. I'll say this, the man can throw one of those stars from a mile away and I swear he will hit his target.

After we told Reaper what happened at the Kings' Club and how the sheriff hit his daughter, he told us to follow him and do surveillance. The man needs to be in jail for hitting his daughter, but since he's a big man on campus, nothing can faze him, and nothing ticks me off more than a man who thinks he can get away with whatever he wants.

I've killed for less.

Knives and I follow the sheriff from the station to the part of town that's known for underground fighting, drugs, and rumor has it, sex trafficking. After experiencing sex trafficking firsthand when visiting Boomer and dismantling a wayward Ruthless chapter, I realize shit like that is more common than we think. Somehow, we find ourselves in the middle of it, and I'm wondering if we need to be some sort of safe haven for people we find in those situations.

"I don't think so, but I'm curious why he's here." It's Johnson and one of his deputies. When the sheriff gets out of his patrol car, he looks around, as does the deputy, to make sure no one has noticed them. I slouch in my seat to hide my face behind the steering wheel. "What the hell is this fucker up to?"

"I say…" Knives' voice is wicked after taking a puff of a cigarette. "…we take the deputy to our little room of joy in the basement and see if we can't get any information out of him."

"You just want to use your ninja star."

"So? I just bought it. Look how pretty it is," he says with too much awe as he flicks the damn thing around in his hand. I scoot toward the window to put some space between me and Knives. I don't feel like getting stabbed.

"Sure, pretty," I mumble and keep my eyes on the two cops walking down the sidewalk until they get to a rundown brick house. I bring the binoculars to my eyes so I can get a closer look. We are too far away to see with the naked eye, so we won't get seen. Knives lifts his binoculars too, and we watch as the sheriff knocks on the door and the deputy, a young kid who looks like he just graduated the academy, looks around nervously. I can see the sweat building on his brows, and the sheriff smacks the kid in the chest, saying something to him that I can't quite decipher.

When the door opens, something tickles in the back of my mind. I know this guy, but I can't place him. He looks strung out on something, and the sheriff hands him a wad of cash before going inside. The deputy stays outside to keep watch. Now is our chance to grab him and take him back to the clubhouse to figure out what kind of cookie jars the sheriff has his hands in, and why he wants Ruthless to talk the fall for it.

"Come on. Let's bring Reaper a gift." I toss the binoculars to the side and put the truck in drive, slowly creeping up to the house. On either side of the street there are gang members, lifting their hands in a gun gesture, telling us they will shoot us. They don't scare me.

Knives rolls down his window and flicks his star out. It's silent, twirling through the air and it pierces the deputy's thigh. He falls to his knee and grabs his leg as blood drips down his khaki uniform. Putting the truck in park, I make sure to take the keys out of the ignition because I don't trust a damn soul on this side of town. I put them in my pocket as Knives and I get out of the truck. When the gang members see our cuts, they disperse immediately and run down the street.

Yeah, that's exactly what I thought.

Knives spins and cackles as we make our way down the sidewalk, empty syringes and used needles gathered on the sand that's supposed to be grass. I crack my knuckles and take my screwdriver from my ear when I squat and run the tip down the deputy's cheek. I just sharpened it, and it cuts flesh beautifully. "Hey there, deputy dipshit," I greet, and the young man tries to pull back. I grip the back of his head and toss him down the steps, and it causes the star lodged in his knee to dig in further until blood makes a trail on the sidewalk.

"What do you want?" he asks, shoulders rising and falling with every rushed gulp of air he takes.

"Answers," I growl as I bring the end of my screwdriver down on the side of his head. He crumbles to the ground, unconscious. "We need to go before the sheriff comes out." I lift the deputy in my arms and throw him in the cab of the truck, making sure to use his cuffs to bind his hands.

"What do you think is going on, Tool?" Knives asks as we pull out of the neighborhood and make our way back to the clubhouse.

I brush my hand over my beard and exhale. "Nothing good, Knives." Whatever the sheriff is involved in, I'm somehow involved in because the guy is coming after me with no care in the world that he's taking an innocent—okay, semi-innocent man—down.

The deputy is groaning when we pull up to the clubhouse, and I knock him out again so he doesn't realize where he's at. I slide my screwdriver over the top of my ear and grab the kid by the ankle and pull him out of the truck. I don't bother picking him up. I hold his foot and drag him across the desert floor, letting his head hit rocks and shit. I don't give a fuck. He deserves pain hanging out with a piece of shit like Sheriff Johnson.

I make my way up the stairs, the deputy's head thudding with every step I take, and Knives prances up the steps, taking out another star and throwing it into the deputy's back. He rolls his head, and his cheeks shake as he groans. "Nothing like the sound of it landing in muscle and hitting bone."

I have some twisted fucking MC brothers. Knives holds the door open as I drag the cop inside, and the first person to notice is Badge.

"What the fuck did you do, Tool?" He stares wide-eyed at the man I'm dragging. "He just got out of the academy."

"Yeah, I figured as much, but I followed your sheriff and he went to a part of town known for illegal things, Badge. Do you know anything about that? Maybe I'm dragging the wrong man on the floor."

"What the fuck did you just say?" Badge takes a step forward, and I drop the deputy's foot. In one quick move, I put Badge in a headlock with my screwdriver at his temple.

"You better think better than that, Badge. I'll make you goddamn Frankenstein with this Philip's head. I find it odd that a cop such as yourself doesn't know more than he lets on." I press the tip of the tool against his skin, and I feel the moment the skin breaks.

"Fuck you! I'd never turn my back on the club."

I push Badge away from me, and a dribble of blood makes its way down his cheek. The cut-sluts are huddled in the corner, all but Becks; she's filing her nails and blowing on them to get the dust off. Her feet are kicked up on the table, paying us know mind. Tongue is out of the shadows, and a few other brothers come in to join the commotion.

Reaper is standing there with his arms crossed, and I point my screwdriver at Badge. "I think it's time this fucker chooses sides. He's either with us, or he's against us. With the shit that's going on, the law can't be trusted."

"I've never given you a reason to doubt me," Badge says, wiping the blood off his face.

"Yet," I finish the sentence for him as I bend down to pick up the deputy and make my way toward the basement. "Prez, we need to talk. Bring the crazy fucks downstairs. Work needs to be done."

"Tongue, Bullseye, Knives. You heard the man; we got work to do," Reaper shouts, and Bullseye pumps his fist in the air.

Tongue throws his blade in the air before catching it with his palm, and Knives dances and spins again while juggling his ninja stars.

"Reaper," Badge's voice causes my nerves to spike. "He's just a kid. Keep that in mind," he says as I open the door and make my way down, his head banging against the wood as I descend.

Thud.

Thud.

Thud.

It happens about fifteen times before I get to the hospital beds, and at the very end, I see Doc checking on Moretti.

He lifts his head when he hears us, and understanding dawns on him when he sees who the men are behind me. When it's all of us together, it can mean nothing good. I continue to drag the deputy, and I turn around to look over my shoulder to find his head is turned to the side, arms up. I peer around Reaper to see a small trail of blood from the star still lodged in his leg.

I place my thumb on the scanner before the metal door slides open and reveal the little room of joy Knives spoke about earlier. There's a metal chair in the middle where a drain is, the floor is inverted for any liquids to drain to easily, and there are all types of weapons on the wall, but we usually stick to what we know.

It's how we've become what we have. I undress the cop until he's naked, and we strap him to the metal chair. Tongue is leaning against the corner, hungry to dish out pain. Knives yanks his star out of the man's leg and then nods when he pushes the guy forward to get the star out of his back. "Almost forgot." He knocks his head with his fist. "Silly me."

Jesus.

Reaper comes in with a bucket of water and throws it on the kid. All too quickly he wakes up and glance around to see himself surrounded by bikers.

"This can go one of two ways," I say. "You give us answers, and we let you live."

"No you won't," he sputters, still spitting out water. He's shivering, and his muscles are taut against the barb wire we have around him, slowly digging into his skin. As long as he stays still, he won't get hurt.

"You won't know until you answer a few questions." Reaper's voice wraps around all of us with power of his command. "Because if you don't talk, you're dead, so what do you have to lose?"

"Wh-what do you want?" His teeth chatter. "I'm new. I don't know a lot, please," he begs and starts to cry.

Fucking come on. Does anyone know how to deal with a little pain?

"Listen…" I get impatient because all I see is Juliette's face with that big red welt on her beautiful flawless cheek, and it sends kerosene through my body. I shove my screwdriver in the guy's shoulder and listen to him scream in agony. A delightful shiver rolls down my spine, tingling my bones, and I inhale the scent of fear and pain. It's been too long since I've felt it and forgot how much I liked it. "I'm not going to beat around the bush. What do you know about the sheriff?" A brief image of me plunging the screwdriver in my father's head surfaces, and I push a little harder on the tool, making the deputy cry out.

"I swear to god, I don't know much. He made me patrol with him tonight; that's it. I swear to god, I swear," he cries, like ugly face cries with his eyes shut and lips turned in a frown.

"What can you tell us?" Reaper asks next. "Believe me, Tool is the tamest of the bunch. You don't want us to work down the line. If Tongue gets ahold of you, you won't ever speak again, kid. So tell us everything."

He nods quickly and licks his lips; his entire body nearly convulses with shivers. The barb wire pricks his skin, and little blood droplets start to flow down his skin. "Okay, please, I swear." He groans when he tilts his head back to deal with the pain flowing through his body. "Sheriff is an ass."

I snort and grip the handle of the screwdriver, threatening to yank it out and force it in another place. "Tell us something we don't know."

"He visits that house three times a week," he says, his stomach quickly bouncing with every fast breath he inhales through his nose. "All the cops know about the place."

I lift my brow to Reaper. "All cops?" I ask again, wondering if Badge knows about it too, and why he hasn't said anything.

"Yeah, all. It's not a good neighborhood. Drugs, money laundering, fights, sex; anything you want, you can get it there."

"At that house?" Tongue drawls, his blade shimmering against the light.

The deputy's eyes round, and another well of tears threaten to spill. What a fucking bitch. Can't handle a little pain; what kind of life did this pussy have? "The house is well known for it," he says just as the smell of urine fills the air.

"Have you been inside?"

He shakes his head. "No, Sheriff always tells me to wait on the porch. I've only been there three times, and every time is the same. Sheriff gives a wad of cash over, and then I don't see him for a few hours. He comes out smelling like sex, sweat, and smoke. That's all I know. I swear to god, that's all I know. I'm new at this. I've only been a cop two weeks. Please."

"You know about us?" Knives asks.

"Everyone knows who the Ruthless Kings are," the young buck says and then closes his eyes, takes a deep breath, and the tears stop. He gets himself together. "If you're going to kill me, do it now; give me that. I've told you everything I know."

Well now that the fear is gone, I don't want to kill him. He took the fun out of it. "Why aren't you shaking like you were before?"

"I know my fate," he says. "Just do it."

"How old you are, kid?" Reaper asks, lightening up a cigarette. "Want one?" I want to laugh as he offers a smoke to the man bound to the chair.

The guy looks confused for a second and shakes his head. "Don't smoke." He stares at Reaper with confusion. "I'm nineteen."

"Holy fuck, kid. Have you even gotten your cock wet?" I

laugh and then yank my screwdriver out of his arm, also pulling out a scream from him that bounces off the walls. It feeds Tongue because he steps out of the shadows and fights himself from going over to the guy and cutting his tongue out.

"I... I've had sex. What the fuck? Kill me; get on with it!" The kid closes his eyes, and I sigh, knowing damn good and well we aren't going to kill some nineteen-year-old boy who was in the wrong place at the wrong time.

"What do you know about the sheriff's daughter? What's his plan with her?"

"I can find out," he says as the idea comes to surface. "I can do whatever you want me to. I'll be your liaison."

"You realize if you fuck us, you're dead, right? You and everyone you love," I threaten.

"I know." He gulps, and his gaze lands on all of us. "I won't let you down."

Huh, maybe if we didn't fuck him too much, we may have just found ourselves a new prospect. "Alright, crybaby." Reaper unwraps the barb wire from around him. "Doc will look at you and clean you up. You're to report to us every day, and if we find out you turned your back on us, I'm not afraid to sick Tongue on you."

"Let me do it, Prez," Tongue begs. "I'll be quick. One slice, just one."

"Keep it in your pants, Tongue. He's just a kid."

"A mouthy one," Tongue pushes off the wall and walks toward the door, stopping in front of the deputy. He growls, showing his

131

teeth to the kid, and the deputy whimpers a bit, pissing himself once again.

I don't blame him. Tongue is a scary sonofabitch, but Tongue won't hesitate to dismember him bit by fucking bit if he doesn't keep his word.

Don't keep your word?

Then you don't keep your tongue; those are the rules he lives by.

I thought I'd see Logan again since the incident with my father, but I haven't. I'm starting to think he's staying away from me, and that doesn't sit well considering my relationship with my father is ruined. It's pointless to stay away now. I'm done waiting around for him. I want answers.

I check myself in the mirror and fluff my hair. I'm wearing a lingerie set under my shirt and shorts. A peek of the black lace can be seen since the V-neck of the shirt exposes it. My hair is in long, thick curls, and I've put on a bit more makeup than usual.

This will be what determines if he wants me or not. After tonight, I'm going to be too tired to care. I'm no one's second choice. I'm no one's uncertainty. Either he's in, or he's out; there can be nothing in between. I know what I want, and I know what I deserve. Being low on someone's priority list isn't something I want for myself.

I won't be a beggar.

I've never been that kind of woman.

Either have me or don't. It's as simple as that. I slip on my red heels and snatch the keys off the coffee table. "Come on, Tyrant." I call for my pooch, and he's hot on my heels. As soon as I open the door, Tyrant bolts out and runs down the steps while jumping next to the car. He loves a car ride. "I'm coming. I'm coming. Cool your jets." I laugh and lock the door.

My instincts scream at me to get out of there, and I look around, taking in my surroundings as I clutch my purse tighter to my body feeling the outline of my gun. An old beat-up Mustang that has seen better days slowly rolls by, and even though I can't see through the window, I can feel their gaze on me. I run to my car, open the door for Tyrant to get in, and once I'm seated, I lock it.

I unzip my purse and dip my hand inside to grab the gun. I twist around to make sure the car is gone, but I keep my finger on the trigger and another to flip the safety off. Tyrant stops growling, and I take that as a cue to leave since the threat is gone.

As I'm driving, I think about Logan and why my dad has such a problem with him. I want to ask Logan, but I honestly don't think he knows. After my dad hit me for the first time, the last thing I want to do is talk to him.

The last rays of the sun fall behind the desert, and all that's left is the pitch black of night and a thousand stars. The desert might be hot, but it's beautiful. The long stretch of road seems to disappear in the dark, and if wasn't for my headlights, the road would be impossible to see.

I take the left down the driveway, and my tires dip, and my car jiggles along with the metal creaking. I get to the gate and breathe a sigh of relief when I see it isn't Pirate at the entrance, but a small scrawny guy with glasses. The patch on his cut says 'prospect' and instead of a road name, it has a simple name, 'Tim.'

"What's your business?" He deepens his voice as he speaks to me, and it takes all I have not to laugh. He puffs out his chest to look bigger, but no matter what this guy does, he will always look like a shrimp. A cute shrimp, but a shrimp, nonetheless.

"I need to see Logan." I notice the moment I mess up because he tilts his head and stares at me like I've lost my mind. Yeah, Tim. I have. I'm at a biker club. I'm obviously not all there. "I mean Tool."

"Oh okay." He shrugs as he steps inside a small hut, probably to click a button because a second later the iron gate slides open.

"Thanks, Tim."

"You're so pretty," he says with bright red cheeks, and then he slams the door to the hut after he catches his slip.

I giggle from his shyness, which isn't expected from a biker, but it's cute. I pull the car forward, and what I see has my eyes going wide. I never noticed when I was at the garage, but the clubhouse is huge. The building itself is old. The architecture looks more like an old saloon which gives it a unique flare.

The car comes to a stop, and I put it in park, taking a deep breath. "We can do this, Tyrant. It would be easier if I had his number, but hopefully that changes tonight."

Tyrant barks in agreeance, and I nod. "Alright, let's do this."

I step foot out of the car, and my heels land in the dirt, and I instantly regret wearing them as they punch through the sand making small holes. Tyrant follows, jumping out of the car and staying by my side as we make our way up the steps. I see the large metal door with dents in it, and I wonder if I need to backtrack and go find my mind that I left somewhere, because no woman in her right mind would willingly be here. Right?

I knock on the door, waiting for someone to answer, and when they don't, I put my hand on the door and turn the knob to find it unlocked. Huh, that's weird. When I open it, I see a crowd of guys shouting at each other. I find Tool in the mix of burly men, but I can't understand him over the shouting. No one has noticed me yet, and as I walk forward I notice a man on the floor. He's alive, but I have no idea how because he's beaten, broken, and bloody.

And his lips are stitched shut.

"Oh my god," I whisper, bringing a shaky hand to my mouth. What rabbit hole did I just fall down?

"Who the fuck was guarding the gate? Who was guarding the damn door? She can't see this!" Reaper yells until he's red in the face, and Tool looks pissed as he stomps toward me. I take a step back from his unexpected charge, but my heel catches in a groove of wood. Right as I fall, Tool catches me, glaring at me with hard

136

eyes.

"What the hell are you doing here, little sparrow?" Logan speaks slow, careful words, as if he's doing all he can not to yell in my face, and his tone doesn't make me feel welcome.

"I wanted to talk to you," I whisper, never taking my eyes off the man on the floor. "What happened to him? Who is he?"

"Take her to your room now, Tool." Reaper's eyes pour hate as he stares at me, and then he grips Tool's cut, stopping him from taking another step toward the direction of his room. "And whenever you're done, meet me in my fucking office because you obviously didn't listen to me."

Tool isn't the kind of man who's scared, but his throat bobs as he swallows, and he gives the guy in charge a small nod as he tugs me toward a hallway, away from the man on the floor. Tool kicks a door open and slings me inside with so much force, my ankle turns to the side, and I can't gather my footing. I stumble back and luckily his bed is behind me because the back of my knees hit the edge of the mattress. With a yelp, I fall back, my head nearly colliding with the wall. Yeti is in the corner, curled up in a ball, and Tyrant lays down next him.

Traitor.

"You can't be here. This is club business, Juliette." Tool peeks out the door before slamming it shut. When he looks at me, he steals my breath from how cold it makes me feel. He usually looks at me with so much warmth and desire, but right now, I feel like an intruder; someone he doesn't trust.

I twist my hands together as I think about my stupid idea to come here. I came here for answers, and the only way to smooth things over is if I ask the questions I need to settle this rift between us. "Logan, will you just explain it to me? I don't want to be on the outside looking in when it comes to you. We've been sidestepping one another. After what we shared—"

"No, don't bring up that night, please."

"Why?" I use the mattress as leverage and push myself up to stand. "I know you felt what I felt." I step forward, needing to be closer to him. "Why are you fighting this?"

"How can I not? Look what you just walked in on? I'm not going to have you hate me in the long run, and that's exactly what will happen if you stay with me. It's how it works. And what about everything your dad has told you?" Somehow, in the middle of his speech, we end up toe to toe, nearly chest to chest. I tilt my chin up to look at him, and the lingering scent of pine and sandalwood creeps into my lungs. Just like that, the sense of feeling at home sets in, and something dangerous swirls in my belly telling me that no matter what Logan says, I'm not going anywhere.

Logan has rooted himself in the marrow of my bones.

I feel the familiar burn of tears in my eyes as I stare down at my hands. I pick the cuticle as my anxiety gets the best of me when I remember the hot sting of my dad's palm against my cheek. "After the other day, I don't believe anything he has ever told me."

The callouses on his fingers scratch my chin, and his touch already feels so familiar. I lean into his hand as he tilts my head up. Our eyes meet, and his dart back and forth between mine, the anger and panic gone, replaced with worry. His lips turn into a frown, and his wild hair falls in his face from the cowlick in the middle of his forehead. I reach to brush it away, but Logan takes a step away from me, leaving me cold.

Logan starts to pace and stares up at the ceiling with his hands on his hips. He's a beautiful man, a beacon of light hidden by a darkness he keeps cloaked over himself for protection. As a shield? I want to know more about Logan McGraw. I want to learn about the darkness to get to that light he keeps away from everyone else.

"That man on the floor..." He points to the door where a beaten man lays behind it. "That man is a nineteen-year-old kid and deputy. One of your father's deputies. We told him a few days ago to do some surveillance. Your dad is in some pretty shady shit. This will be the second person who's come to our door with their mouth stitched shut. We never should've told him to do surveillance. Fuck!" he screams, kicking his dresser so hard his boot punches through, creating a massive hole. A retro-eighties lamp falls and shatters on the floor, and a few drawers open from the force. "Just a fucking kid, and I went too hard on him when I—"

"When you what?" I ask, and in two wide strides he's in front of me. He takes the screwdriver from his ear. My mouth is dry, turning to cotton when he spins the sharp metal between his fingers. It shines clean and almost hypnotizes me.

"When I stabbed him with this screwdriver to get information on your dear old daddy. I drove it right into his shoulder to get the answers I wanted," he says, watching the screwdriver before looking at me and pointing at my shoulder. He's waiting to see how I'll react, but I just remember the tip of that tool being underneath my chin while it's been in someone's flesh. "Are you afraid of me, little sparrow?" His voice turns dark, promising pain and misery, but I know he's only trying to scare me.

"You'd never hurt me."

"How can you be so sure? Hurting people is my job. How do you know I won't ever drive this through your skull?"

"Because you don't hurt women," I say, reminding him of the words he first told me.

"I would if I had to," he admits. "If that woman was a threat." I know what he's trying to do, but no matter what he says, his eyes and his body go against the strong vibrato of his voice. Logan's attempt at his truth is a lie.

"Am I a threat, Logan?" My voice is stronger than it should be, but I'm doing my best to remain in control of my fear. There are two things I know about Logan.

He'll never hurt me.

But he'll hurt anyone else if he has to.

"You're a threat to me." Logan's wide throat bobs as he swallows, breaking our eye contact. He looks toward the floor, the most uncertain I've ever seen him look.

"Logan." I lay my palm on his chest, and the white-knuckle

grip he has on the weapon he's so attached to loosens, and his arm falls between us. I bring my other hand up and slide it through his palm, taking the screwdriver away from him. He tightens his grip again, as if he's afraid to be apart from it. "It's okay. You don't need this with me, Logan. Let me have it." I slip my fingers around the handle, and slowly his fingers relax, allowing me to take it from him.

I have a feeling that is a big step. If he were a knight, the screwdriver would be his sword, and a knight never goes anywhere without his blade.

"Juliette." My name is a groan as he speaks. "We can't. Your dad… You'll hate me for what I have to do. I can't have you—"

"Shh—" I place my fingers against his lips, debating if I want to know more about my father, or if I want to silence Logan with a kiss and remind him how good it can be between us. I love my father, but I'll never forgive him for hitting me, for being so vicious against Logan—an innocent man. Whatever Logan has on my dad, I'm not ready to know yet because I have a feeling it will ruin me. "I don't want to know."

"You need to before you make any decisions about me," he says as he cups my face, bringing his lips closer to mine. His thumb rubs against my bottom lip, tugging it down and rubbing from side to side as if he's debating on what to do about my mouth.

Kiss it.

He bends down, his lips a breath away, and I smell a hint of beer lingering on his tongue. A little closer.

"Tool!" Reaper's voice interrupts us along with a loud pound of his fist. Both Logan and I sigh, and he lays his forehead against mine and runs his fingers down my arm until he's at the hand that holds his sword.

To some it may just be a screwdriver, but to Logan, it's how he protects himself and the ones he loves.

He pulls it free from my hand and brings his lips to my forehead. "Stay in here. We'll talk when I come back."

"Where are you going? What's going to happen?" His boot thuds on the wooden planks against the floor, and it sounds like he's walking to his death. I grab his vest, and he turns his head over his shoulder until his chin is resting on the curve of his muscle, lifting a groomed black brow at me. "What's he going to do to you?"

"Nothing I don't deserve. I'll be back." He walks out of my hold, leaving me to grab nothing but a ghost and the fleeting stare of the skull on his back.

"Are you fucking kidding me!" Reaper's roar is directed at me while I kneel on the ground in the chapel. The long desk that we all sit around is pushed against the wall, and my brothers surround me. Reaper rips off my cut and tosses it against Bullseye's chest, and he flinches, not expecting to have to catch it.

I'm in so much fucking trouble.

Reaper grips my neck and jerks my head back. "One rule, Tool. One. Don't fuck the sheriff's daughter. You couldn't keep your dick away, could you? Do you know how bad this can get for us? We have a war on our hands, Tool. A war, and you're fucking the enemy!" he screams in my left ear, causing it to ring. His breath is warm puffing against my cheek as he debates how he's going to attack. "Come on, Tool!" he hisses, and spits flies and lands on my face, wet and hot, almost like it's a toxin trying to burn flesh skin off.

"I'm sorry, Prez." It's all I say because again I've fucked up beyond belief. He doesn't need to know that I haven't fucked her because I've done other things. I want to fuck her. I want more with her than I've ever had, but I know I need to let her go.

I just don't think I can.

"Take your shirt off," Reaper orders, taking a blade from Tongue's hands.

Tongue usually looks happy when he gets to see someone cut up and bleeding, but right now, he can't even look at me.

I reach behind my head and grab the collar of my shirt, yanking it off to give him what he wants. "Is the kid okay?" I ask about the deputy who was left at the entrance of our driveway just like Ghost was, then I toss my shirt on the ground. I know what everyone sees; not even all the tattoos can cover the cigarette burns my father left all over my body. Numerous scars on my torso and back. The tattoos make me feel more confident since the scars can't be directly seen, but puffy circles of scar tissue are raised, and tattoos can't hide that.

"Doc is looking him over," Bullseye says, and Reaper glares at him for speaking out of turn.

"Don't," Reaper snarls through tight teeth. He bends down and keeps his voice so low that only I can hear him. "I have to make an example. I can't look weak in front of my men, and you've made me look weak more than once, Tool. I've put off the punishment for Sarah because I knew it was an accident. This, me telling you to say away from the sheriff's daughter; I thought that would be easy for you. You could have any piece of ass, any cut-slut, so why; what's so special about her?"

My eyes land on a few of my brothers that are around me, Tongue, Knives, and Pirate. I notice Pirate doesn't have a bottle of rum in his hand like usual, and his typically pale skin is a normal color.

"We've been through a lot together, Tool. You're still the guy who holds my trust, but I need to know what the hell I have to get ready for if you don't plan on letting her go." Reaper waits for my answer, and I honestly have no idea what to tell him.

I want to keep seeing her, but I also don't want her to be burdened with a man like me. Having her is a huge gain for me, but her having me? I'll only and will forever be someone dimming her light. I'm nothing but a loss for her.

"I'm not going to let her go," I say, daring to meet his flaming brown eyes. "She's ol' lady material for me, Reaper."

A few murmurs of surprise roll around me from my brothers. They don't see me with many women, and it's because I keep my dick out of the public eye. It's why I don't fuck sluts in the clubhouse and bring a woman into my room.

Usually.

Juliette is in there right now.

"You're an idiot, Tool. The sheriff's daughter?"

"Coming from the man married to someone who's nineteen." I close my eyes when I realize my slip up. I may have just signed my death sentence. "Reap—" Before I can finish saying his name, his fist connects to my jaw with so much force, my back hits the hardwood, and my elbow snaps one of the floorboards in half. I groan, and Reaper's boot lands on my chest, keeping pinned me to the ground. "I deserved that. I'm sorry."

"For disobedience and not following my command, you're going to be marked with a warning."

Oh fuck. No, no, no, not this.

"Reaper," I choke, begging him with my eyes to reconsider this. I know that I have to do this because I deserve it. I'm lucky he didn't strip me of my patch when I punched Sarah in the face. It was a complete accident. I still can't believe she jumped in front of Boomer and took that hit. For months, Reaper has been waiting for the perfect punishment because he didn't want to punish me in front of everyone.

"Once this is done, we move forward." Reaper places the tip of the blade over my heart, and I take a few deep breaths trying to mentally prepare myself for the pain. Reaper has a three-strike rule before he cuts out a member's heart.

He engraves a heart on the chest.

Next, if the member disobeys again, he carves an arrow through it.

The third time, that's when someone takes their last breath and he holds someone's bloody soul in his palm.

"Give me a lighter."

Oh, yeah, he heats the blade too making sure that it scars. It's a reminder I have to look at every day for the rest of my life of how

I failed my best friend.

He stares at me like this hurts him more than it will me. Yeah, I highly doubt that. Reaper's hair is hanging in his face, and when Bullseye flicks the light on, an iridescent glow flickers in his pupil. Reaper places the blade over the fire, letting it heat until the metal turns black from the fumes. He flips the knife over making sure the metal gets nice and scalding to ruin my flesh with, and a scold sweat breaks over my body.

Instead of Reaper, it's my father standing over me after beating me until I can't move, relighting the cigarette every time he hits my skin. I can already smell my burning flesh. I can't bitch out. I have to do this.

I don't struggle.

I don't beg for mercy.

I lay there, waiting for my punishment like I always have.

Reaper bends down and removes his boot, his brows pinch together, and we share a look, one that's full of apology and acceptance. Without warning, he presses the knife above my heart and starts to cut. I keep my screams inside, not wanting the members to see their VP bitch and moan over pain when I've experienced worse.

Still, hot metal searing my skin isn't the greatest feeling.

I tense, squeezing my eyes shut and take deep, gasping breaths, almost like I'm hyperventilating, but breathing so fast and hard helps with the pain. The tip of the blade curves up then down, and sweat drips off me in puddles as my body reacts to the fire being placed on my skin. Reaper twists the knife, bringing it up to another curve before bringing it to the starting point.

It's done.

He removes the knife from my skin, my aching, burning flesh and the smell makes me want to vomit. The bile works its way up my throat, but I swallow it down and roll over onto my hands and knees, shaking my head to try to clear the dizziness.

"Don't make me put that arrow on you, Tool. Don't fucking make me." Reaper hauls me up to my feet, and my nostrils flare with the intensity of my breathing as I look my President in the eye.

"You won't have to." Blood drips down my chest and the ridges of my abs. My shoulders rise and fall, my skin is trembling from the shock. Reaper stretches out his hand, telling me he's ready to put it all behind us.

A flash of my father takes Reaper's place, and I close my eyes and try to pull my sanity together.

It isn't him. Reaper isn't him. This was a different punishment. You're fine. You've proved yourself. That's the difference.

"Tool?" Reaper barks my name to bring me out of my daze, and when I open my eyes, expecting to see an image of my drunk father, I see Reaper and his scowl.

It's hard to believe, but what a relief. My father is dead. He can't hurt me anymore. I made sure of that.

"I'm fine," I say, walking over to where my shirt is on laying on the floor and pick it up. "My cut? Do I get to keep my patch?" The words are rough as they leave my parched throat. If Reaper takes my VP status, I'll be fucking devastated. This MC is everything to me; being Reaper's right-hand man means everything to me.

Reaper rips my cut from Bullseye's hands and throws it to me. "Tool, you'll be my VP until your last fucking breath or mine. You don't have to worry about that. Go rest for the night, all of you." He slowly circles to look at everyone. "We will have a long day tomorrow. The sheriff picked a fight with the wrong people. Badge? Stay behind. I want to talk to you."

Everyone heads toward the door, a languid thunder of boots ready for their freedom. I'm the first one to pass Badge. I don't think he knows what's going on with the Sheriff, and I should have given him slack, but I stand by what I said.

Either be a cop or be in an MC.

He can't have both, and he can't be both. For this purpose right here. The water is too fucking mucky, and whatever Reaper is about to talk to him about, it can't be worse than having a heart carved in your chest; warning you that any more mistakes is one step closer to having your soul reaped.

I pat Badge on the back, and a few guys do the same to me, including Poodle. The biggest pain in the ass that I have here.

"Took balls to lay there while he had that knife to your chest and not scream or say a peep. I can still smell your flesh, and I think your chest is smoking," Poodle coughs and waves at it. I look down to see what he's talking about, and I snort. Damn, it fucking is. No wonder it hurts so bad. My skin is cooking.

"Balls, aye, but not bigger than mine!" Skirt slams his hand on my shoulder and shakes me. Since my chest is so damn sensitive, my heart feels like it's about to fall out of my sternum and onto the floor.

"Thanks, guys." I don't have the energy to give them shit. I just want to get cleaned up and lay down. When I enter the main room, all the cut-sluts are there waiting, and Becks is just chilling on the couch, watching TV.

"I can make you feel better, Tool," Millie purrs, sliding her hands up my arms. "I can kiss it better." She puckers her lips, and I cringe internally thinking about where those lips have been. For instance, around half of the MC's cocks, and I'm not about sloppy one hundredth, or whatever the hell it's called.

"No thanks, Millie. You know my rules." I have a woman waiting on me in my room who I'll risk my life for. I'm not giving that up for a used-up piece of ass. No offense to Millie, but that's exactly what she is. She throws herself for anyone hoping to gain that property patch, but I don't know when the cut-sluts will get it through their minds that they're just time passers for us until the right woman comes along.

"Fine, but it would be so good." She winks and sashays her flat ass back behind the bar.

I curl my lip and pivot on my heel to enter the hallway that leads to my room when Poodle stands in my way. "Poodle, not now, man," I groan.

"Poodle? Where are... Oh, hi, Tool," Melissa, one of the

girls we saved from the sex trafficking incident in Jersey comes out of Poodle's room.

"You okay?" Poodle's fun tone is gone, the one he constantly uses when he speaks to her. "Bad dream?" he asks, and she gives me a quick look before her cheeks turn red, and she hurries back in the room.

"Poodle, if you got something to say, say it. I got shit I still need to take care of tonight." I start the journey down the hall, staring at my bedroom door at the end of it.

"Keep your mutt away from my Lady; you hear me? Both of your mutts," he warns. There's the Poodle I know and love. "She has a big show coming up, and I won't have your dogs ruining her big break."

"Oh, Jesus Christ, Poodle. Again with the damn shows? And if Yeti wants to get it on with Lady, and she's willing, who am I to stop love?"

"You better! I swear, Tool. I'll—"

I open my bedroom door and slam it in his face, not wanting to deal with him. I lay my head against the wood and take a few deep breaths, locking the deadbolt in place.

"This isn't over!" he shouts, causing me to smile a bit. The bickering is never over between us. I take a moment to catch my breath before turning around, hoping to find Juliette when I see my bed is empty.

Fuck, did she leave? "Juliette? Juliette!" I hurry to the restroom to see her drying her face with a towel, dressed in one of my shirts. It's a Ruthless Kings shirt, black, a bit newer than a lot of my other shirts, and it's way too big on her, but damn, a shirt has never looked better. "You're still here," I say with relief.

She smiles, but it fades fast when her eyes land on my chest. "Oh my god, Logan!" She runs to me and reaches out to touch my chest, but she doesn't because she's afraid she'll hurt me.

Her touch could never hurt me.

It's the only thing that reminds me I'm able to feel something other than hate.

"Sit on the bed. I saw a first-aid kit under your sink; let me take care of you," she says and shoos me toward the bed. I sit, and she's satisfied that I don't argue with her, as she opens the cabinet door under the sink and rummages through whatever goodies are down there.

Let me take care of you.

But how do I take care of you, Juliette?

The silence is a bit awkward as I clean his wound. I'm not good with silence. I always have to be the one who fills it with something, anything. I wet a bandage with rubbing alcohol and gently start to clean away the dead, burnt skin. My eyes water, but not from the fumes of the alcohol, but from the idea that someone would do this to Logan. I want to know why, but I don't know how to ask because I have a feeling it's my fault.

So I do what I always do when I'm upset or nervous. I sing. I keep the Nora Jones song quiet and soft, careful not to be too loud. I don't want to annoy anyone, and as I clean the perfectly carved heart on Logan's beautiful chest, I realize how carnal the people must be to live day to day in an organization like this.

"You have a beautiful voice," Logan says after a few minutes of me poking at his chest.

"Sorry, I'll be quiet. I sing to fill the silence." I turn away and drop the bandage in the trash can. My hair falls over my face and hides my embarrassment. I dig through the red box of the first-aid kit and pluck out another piece of gauze.

His hand lands on top of mine when I reach for the hydrogen peroxide, completely covering my small finger with his wide palm. "I never want you to stop singing. I could listen to you for the rest of my life. Continue, please."

Logan doesn't seem like the kind of guy to say please. It almost sounds foreign coming from a man who looks like him. Logan strikes me as the kind of guy who demands what he wants. The kind of man who would make me sing, not simply ask me to.

"I-I don't know." My face is as hot as freaking hot sauce. "I don't sing in front of people."

"I'm not people, little sparrow."

"Why do you call me that?" I finally ask. "Is it because of my nose or something? Do I have a beak nose?" I cover my nose with my hand and gasp, blocking it so he can't see it.

He tosses his head back and laughs until he's wincing, holding his chest from the pull and tug of the skin. "You have a beautiful nose. When I first met you, I thought you were a princess, but the more I heard your voice, the more I thought you sounded like a song and song sparrows always have the prettiest tune. And now I know you can sing like that; it just proves that I'm right. Come on. Sing for me."

"Logan—"

"My heart is in your hands. Let me hear that voice." His

knuckles brush against my chin, and when I glance up from the black seared edges of the new mark on his chest, I see the warmth shining in his eyes.

My resolve breaks. it always does when it comes to Logan. I start disinfecting his wound again. "You won't make fun of me?"

"Baby, you could sound like a damn crow, and I'd still think it's the best thing I've ever heard."

I giggle with a shake of my head, causing my hair to fall over my shoulders. "Why? That's terrible."

"Because it's coming from you, Juliette."

I let out a shaky breath and toss the used gauze in the trash can. My nerves are fluttering around in my stomach like a swarm of freaking bats. Forget the bees; my nerves have upgraded. I clear my throat and reach for the tube of bacitracin. I decide to go with another Nora Jones song, my favorite artist in the entire world. My mom always put on Nora Jones' album for me when I went to sleep, and her music is the best to sing when I need to be soothed, so I hope it's the same for Logan.

While I'm singing, Logan closes his eyes as I pick and prod at his chest. Before I cover it, I want to make sure that I get all of the burnt skin off. It looks so painful and raw. I want to punch Reaper in the face for doing this to him, but I don't want to make things worse than I already have.

The song comes to an end while I'm laying a square bandage on his impressive pectoral. How is a man this muscular? If I wanted to, I could wash my clothes against his stomach because he has washboard abs.

Washboard. Abs.

I'm going to have to take a picture so I can look at his body whenever I want.

"There. All done," I say on a sigh. As I step away, Logan's fingers snag around my wrist and stop me from taking another step.

"I like your hands on me." He pulls me to him again, and I'm closer than I was before when I bandaged his chest. Logan controls my hand and places them on his pecs again, and his chest rises and falls while a low hum runs through his body. "Yeah, like that. I love your touch, and I love this—" He strokes the middle of my throat, telling me he likes my voice. "You sound like a mixture of Janis Joplin and Nora Jones. It's beautiful. You are beautiful. I don't want to touch you because I'm afraid I'll ruin you. That's what I do, Juliette. I ruin."

I slide my palms up his neck. His beard is softer than I thought, and I caress the soft locks, loving how it feels as the strands glide between my fingers. He moans as I massage his face, enjoying how his eyes close, and the vibrations in his throat tickles my palms.

"Feel good?" I say with a smile, then tug on his chin hair.

"Are you kidding? It's your hands. Anything you do to me will feel good."

I lick my lips for a second, debating if I want to take the chance that I know I want to take, but I'm afraid I'll get rejected.

Everyone deals with rejection, right? It's part of life. I double check to make sure his eyes are shut, and my gaze drops to his lips. They're plump and pink, hidden behind a thick frame of black hair. I stop rubbing his cheeks and gently cup his defined, square jaws and lean in, taking a leap of faith as I press my lips against his.

It's a long peck; no tongue, no urgency. Just something soft and sweet. I have a feeling he hasn't felt anything sweet in a long time. Reluctantly, I tear my lips away, my eyes fluttering open to see his lips still slightly parted and puckered for me.

"How did that feel?" I hardly recognize the sound of my voice with how hoarse it is.

"Like a fucking dream I never want to wake up from." In a blink of an eye, he grabs my face and smashes our lips together. Soft and sweet is gone, and passionate and urgent has taken its place. We breathe down each other's throats, living only to taste one another. My lips part as I whimper when his tongue slides against mine.

"Fuck me, I can't get enough of you," he says on a frustrated growl, and his hands slide down my body, grip my ass, and lift me on to his lap. "This ass." He squeezes my cheeks in his palms and then rocks me against his hard cock. "You're perfect."

"Your chest," I say between ragged breaths. Trying to get control of my body is impossible when his fingers are digging deep into my flesh, gripping, squeezing, pulling me against his erection. My clit drags against the thick shaft since the only barrier between us are my panties.

"My heart is full," he replies, taking my mouth again in a kiss that makes my body so hot, a flood of cream soaks my panties as my lust grows with every stroke of his tongue against mine and every slide of his cock between my sheath.

"I don't want to hurt you." He tilts my head back after the words leave my lips, and Logan bites down on my neck, sending sharp stings through my nerves. My hands tangle in his hair, and the shaved side is like prickly bristle hairs against my palm while his long side is like strands of silk. I thought the longer black locks would be rough or coarse like him, but they aren't; they're soft, like the heart he hides.

"Oh, little sparrow, you should be worried about me hurting you." In one swift motion, Logan flips me to the bed by the hold he has on my ass, and now I'm staring up at him, watching him, watching me while his hands ever so slowly lift his shirt off my body. "The things I want to do to you." The words end on a primal growl, and his fingers dig into my hips as hard as they can. Hard enough to bruise, and I guess in a way, it hurts me.

And in the morning, I'll be able to see his marks on me.

"What do you want to do?" I ask, my breaths coming out harsh as he lowers his head to my abdomen, hovering his lips just below my belly button.

He presses a soft kiss and then lets out an ironic chuckle, skimming his hands up my ribcage. His shaky breaths make my skin bead and he pauses, closing his hungry eyes as if he's trying to stop himself from tearing me apart. "I think the better question is"—his muscular throat bobs as he speaks—"what don't I want to do to you?"

An audible gulp sounds, loud and embarrassing.

He chuckles, dark and menacingly, and the room drops in temperature. My blood boils when he cups my breasts under the shirt, bringing his mouth to my ear as he whispers, "Sounds like you're afraid now."

I shake my head and circle my arms around his neck, whispering, "Only afraid that I won't please you."

He grabs my chin and forces me to meet his eyes. His brows furrow angrily, and his lips pinch together, creating wrinkles around his mouth where his laugh lines are. "You please me more just by being here with me, more than anyone ever has. Whatever we do, whatever we share, it will be more than anything I've experienced. I don't think you understand"—he brushes his nose along my cheek—"how you've turned my world upside down." My brown hair falls over my shoulder as it flows out from the inside of the shirt when Logan tugs the extra-large material over my head.

Logan's eyes roam my body, staring me at me like he's never seen me naked before, but he has. His hand lays in the middle of my chest. One, two, three seconds pass before he trails his finger down the middle of my abdomen. "So soft," he awes, brushing his fingers over me like a paintbrush against a blank canvas.

As I watch him map me with his touch, his tattooed hands

against my plain, unmarked skin, I suppose that's what we are.

He's the paintbrush.

I'm his canvas.

And with every stroke he makes along the nerve endings on my skin, the closer we become to creating the masterpiece that is us.

I don't think he's ever heard this, but he's beautiful. I'm sure he's heard handsome, sexy, and hot, but I don't think anyone has really looked into his eyes and seen the vulnerability of his soul he keeps locked away, so deep that it can never be touched.

Except right now, I'm getting to experience the softness he traps inside him that no one else can see, and it's beautiful.

Logan McGraw is beautiful.

Without saying another word, he leans down and kisses me, taking his time to trace my lips with his tongue before diving inside my eager mouth. My hands press gently against his chest, and he sits up, letting me run my hands down the exquisite sculpture that is his body.

He is art.

And he deserves to be appreciated.

I untether the button on his jeans and slide down the zipper, and the grinding teeth separating unlock something inside me. I only want to pleasure him and make him feel good. I have an inkling that he doesn't get to feel good too often. One of his large hands cups the back of my head as I work his jeans down his hips.

On either side of his hips are geometric tattoos, dipping in a

V that leads to his cock. It feels big, really big, and I'm not sure how to handle the monster, but I'll try. I gulp loudly when I see the base of him come to view, surrounded by a thick patch of black hair. Before I can pull his jeans the rest of the way down his legs, he stands and does the work for me.

The jeans go somewhere. I don't look for them or anything as he slings them over his shoulder because my eyes lock onto his cock and heavy balls hanging between his legs.

"Oh, wow," I say on a half moan, half croak, half gasp. It doesn't sound sexy because a train of nerves has smashed against me, swaying the confidence I felt just milliseconds ago. He wraps a hand around himself and strokes the long, thick length.

It's also tattooed.

And it's pierced. Holy shit—it's pierced. The head has a thick hoop coming from it, and then rods pierce his shaft all the way down.

He must be nine inches and a wrist wide with thick veins pumping it full of blood and lust.

I gulp, again.

"It's a Jacob's Ladder, my innocent little sparrow, and a Prince Albert. It feels good when you rub me, but I promise"—he falls forward, and his cock settles between my shaking thighs as he cages my head in with his strong arms, teasing his lips over mine. "When I'm inside you"—he starts to rock his hips, and the tip of his pierced cock hits my clit, making me moan—"it's going to rub so many spots inside you, and I can't wait to feel you come around me."

"Logan…" His name is a pathetic whine in my throat. I'm already close to falling apart, and he hasn't even touched my pussy yet. I'm so pathetic. I've never experienced burning like this. Inside me it physically hurts, and if I don't feel him inside me soon, I just might die.

I'm consumed by her.

Her smell, her taste, her skin, and the closer I get to her, I realize it isn't close enough. I want to ravage her, own her in every way. She's possessed me. I need more. I need more of her. This isn't enough.

"I need you now, Juliette. I can't wait any longer. Next time, I'll lick that pretty pussy until you're screaming my name, and then I want your mouth around me, but right now? I need to be inside you."

"Yes, Logan, please!" She squeezes her tits, and I can't help myself. I lunge forward and take a peaked rosy nipple into my mouth, trying to gather the milky flesh along with it. I want all of it.

She's delicious.

I flick my tongue one last time over the sweet morsel and kiss my way up her neck until I steal her mouth in a desperate kiss. I do my best to distract her as I dip my fingers inside her panties and feel her wet folds parting for me.

I groan when her slick soaks me, teasing my cock with the promise of her tight heat. I bring my fingers to my mouth and hum in appreciation when her honey coats my taste buds. Yanking her panties aside, I grab the thick base of my cock with my wet fingers and guide it to her dripping wet hole where white creamy cum is leaking out of her. I can't wait to feel her drenching my cock.

Her hole tightens around me, and a gasp leaves Juliette. I lay over her perfect curvy body and caress her sides, up and over her heavy tits, until I have ahold of her jaw. Our eyes lock, and I'm enchanted by her green eyes, lost in the magical forest hidden beneath the depths.

"Logan."

She says my name, coated in nerves and a twinge of fear, clutching her hands on my shoulders until her nails dig into my skin.

"I got you. It's okay." I slide in deeper, and my mouth drops open when more of her tight channel grips me. She's breathing heavy, whimpering, shutting her eyes to push through the pain. "Look at me," I demand, and she instantly pops her eyes open, wide and innocent.

When I hit her barrier, I grunt, wanting to just punch through and fuck her like the wild instinct ferociously pumping inside me, but I don't. I hold back and start with shallow thrusts, gliding the few inches of my cock in and out.

She relaxes with every stroke, and suddenly small moans of pleasure are escaping her. Her pussy gets impossibly wetter. I moan as I curl over her, bringing our lips so close that a single breath would push us together, but I want to see her face when I plunge inside her, and she's stretched full of me.

Instead of punching through her virginity, I use the dripping nectar of her cunt soaking my shaft and slide in smoothly besides a slight tug. I expect a painful cry to join my pleasurable moan, but one never comes. Her hands run down the curve of my back until they cup my ass, pulling me closer and filling her tight cunt with my length even more.

"Oh god, Logan." She tosses her head back and forth before biting her lip. "You feel so good. You're so … thick," she moans, and I nearly come right then.

Hearing her say that my cock feels good strokes my ego. Every man loves hearing it, and a lot of times, women just say it to say it, but not Juliette; not during her first time.

"Your pussy was made for my cock, Juliette." I rear back then push forward, past her tight walls until I hit the tip of her womb. My Jacob's Ladder rubs underneath my shaft while also giving her more sensations, and I can't hold back anymore.

"Harder, Logan. Harder."

"You're reading my mind, little sparrow." I lift off her body, grab her right leg, and place her foot on my shoulder. "Oh, fuck, yes," I hiss, tossing my head back onto my shoulders from the

165

change of position. My punishing rhythm makes her tits bounce, and her lips are parted, just waiting for something to fill it. "Juliette, you feel so goddamn good." My sack slaps against her ass with every fervent curl of my hips to send my cock into a plummeting chaos.

Sweat drips into my eyes and causes a slight sting from the salt. I glance down to stare at my cock sliding in and out of her, and it's a vision I can never forget. Her virgin blood coats me along with her sweetness, a divine wine that will taste better than any drink.

My hands grab onto her hips and force them down on my cock harder, and Juliette screams my name again, and no doubt the rest of the house can hear her. "That's right. Let everyone know who's fucking you, little sparrow. This is my cunt, isn't it? Mine. I took your virginity, and that means you belong to me. Tell me."

"Yes, Logan," she moans.

I rear back and slam into her harder. "Again."

"I'm all yours and only yours," she says, holding her arms above her head while she watches me fuck her.

"Again," I growl, using her words as fuel to pump myself into her harder in hopes she explodes around my cock and sucks me dry.

"Logan, Logan! I'm yours. Fuck, I'm only yours! Yes!" Her back arches off the bed when the first spasm of her orgasm shakes her. Her breasts jiggle, and her stomach tenses along with her sweet cunt, clasping around my thickness. A gush of fluid runs down my cock, and I'm greeted by the whites of her eyes as they roll back to her head.

I yank my cock from her wet constraint and flip her over onto her stomach, pressing her head into the pillow as I slide back in without that damn barrier in my way. "Oh, now this is a fucking view." I slap each round, bubbled cheek with my hands and grip the meat while I pound into her from behind. She muffles her moans into the pillow, and I yank it away from her. "I want to hear you."

"Logan, it's too much. You feel too good. I'm so sensitive."

"Give me another."

"I can't!" she defies me, but her body defies her because with every stroke I give her, she's pressing her ass into me, wanting more.

She's hungry for me.

"You'll give me another before I fill you up." I wrap my hand around her hair and pull her back, manipulating her head until her mouth is close to mine again. "You want that, don't you? You want to be full of me, dripping with my cum." I rub my lips over the shell of her ear, and a shaky breath leaves me when I think of painting her walls with my seed. I'm too close now. I reach down and pinch her clit, rolling the nerves between my fingers.

She slams her fist against the wall, bucking against me like an untamed mare as her pussy sucks me in with every wave and spasm her body gives. I use my weight to push her flat on the bed, and I lay against her back while I plant myself inside her, roaring her name on my release. With every strong jet that leaves my shaft, I pull back before the stream leaves me before rooting my cock inside her for the next searing wave of cum to leave my body.

"Take every fucking drop, Juliette. Every damn drop. You're going to take it all for me," I tell her, lazily sliding in and out of her swollen deflowered heat. She's so wet from our combined juices that I never want to pull my cock out. I press a kiss against the back of her neck, and the salty goodness almost makes me harden again.

I turn her head with the palm of my hand and give her a languid, messy kiss. Our tongues collide, soft and sweet, just like the sound of her voice. With a shit ton of regret, I break the kiss and roll us to our sides, keeping my cock lodged inside her. I can feel my come leaking out of her and for some reason, a maddening anger takes over.

I want her bound to me. I can't give up something that feels this good. I can't let her leave me. She's the only good in my life. She outshines all the rage, hate, and misery I feel on a day to day basis. She's my fucking home and the only good part left in my heart.

Gathering the juices off her thigh, I bring my cum to her clit and start to swirl.

"Oh no, Logan." She grips my wrist in warning, and her body trembles and squirms as she tries to get away. "It's too much. I'm too sensitive. You're going to make me come again."

I nip her ear. "I know. I just love hearing you come for me, little sparrow. You sound so beautiful. You hit the highest note when you scream my name, and I want to hear it again." I rub harder and faster on her clit, and now my cock is ready again, but I don't move. I won't need to.

"Logan." Her body bends from the quick rush of her impending orgasm.

"Juliette!" My body breaks, my sack drawing up tight again. I've never come too fast before, but I do for Juliette. Her pleasure is my pleasure.

Her thighs clamp together and my name, once again, is a harmonic note ringing through the air. I grunt one final time, filling her with another smaller load of my seed. It's barbaric, to take her bare and raw like this, hoping like hell her womb takes me.

I don't know the first thing about being a father. I don't even know if I'll be good at it considering who I am. She makes me want to be better. She makes me want to try to reach for something other than the misery inside me.

Even if I know misery will always be a part of me, I need it to survive just like I need Juliette.

"Wow," she says on a deep exhale, somehow falling even more limp on the mattress. "That was... I can't believe I waited so long to do that."

I growl like a rabid animal, flipping her over onto her back. In a blink of an eye, I have my screwdriver under her chin again while I'm biting at her bottom lip. "You better be glad you waited so long. I would have had to kill every asshole who had been with you."

She laughs thinking I'm joking, but the crazy glint in my eye has her smile falling. "You're serious?"

"Very," I grumble in unease when I think of her with someone else besides me. "You're mine, Juliette. I don't fuck without protection. I don't fuck bare. I do with you, though, and that's how we are always going to fuck; do you understand? Nothing will be between us." I sound like a goddamn maniac, but the insanity keeps pouring from my mouth, and my weapon that has seen the inside of more skulls than screws to tighten, run, down her neck to her breasts, and the cold steel causes her nipple to bead. "You like that, little sparrow?"

She nods rapidly, and I slide my screwdriver down her stomach, over the ribs, then back up over the mountains of her lush tits.

"You may not know it, but you're just as fucked up as me. The difference is it's all in your head, little sparrow. I live what's in my head." My cock is raging again, and I don't know how. When I see that she isn't afraid of me when the tool in my hand is what shaped me as a man, lust flares again.

I go to toss the screwdriver on the floor, but she stops me in time, bringing the screwdriver underneath her chin again. "Fuck me like you hate me, Logan."

I throw the damn thing on the ground and take her mouth with mine. "No."

"Why not?"

"I can never hate you. I can't even pretend to hate you, Juliette."

"Why not, Logan? You know you want to."

I do want to, but I want to love her more. While that might not be a big deal to some, it is for me. It means for the first time in my life something outweighs the bad inside me.

"Because you're too good to hate, little sparrow. Even the souls that are damned like mine know that." I lay my forehead against her, and for the first time in my fucking life, I ease my cock in and out, kissing her to show her how much I love her. It hits me like a sledgehammer that I'm making love to her.

She's my safe haven.

I'm her damnation.

And I hope I don't end up dragging her to the depths of my hell.

I wake up the next morning, sore and aching in every single place on my body. Tool and I had sex all night. I've only had two hours of sleep according to the clock. I stretch, and my arm hits a rock-solid back. I turn to my left and grin to myself when I see a large skull staring at me. I trace the tattoo with my finger, stroking the cracks in the skull and the darkness around the eye sockets.

"That feels good," Tool mutters sleepily, and if I wasn't so sore, I would want to fuck him again. That sleepy voice is sexy.

I press a kiss to his shoulder, and my lips rub over something puffy and circular. I lean back and touch it with my finger and now that I'm aware, I see these small circles all over his back. "What are these?"

"I don't like to talk about it."

"You can talk to me, Logan. I won't judge you."

"Yes, you will. If I tell you what I did, you'll run out that door, and I won't ever see you again."

"Give me the benefit of the doubt, Logan. I want to know about you. I want to know you. All of you. Every good and bad part."

"That's the thing, little sparrow." He flips over and grabs my wrist mid-air. "I don't have a good part in me."

"I don't believe that for one second, Logan. Not one. Please, did someone do this to you?" I run my hands down his chest, and that's when I see hundreds of the circles. How did I miss them before? My eyes sting with tears as a horrible thought occurs. "Did someone do this to you, Logan?"

"Let it go, Juliette!" he raises his voice at me, but I don't back down.

"Logan."

"Fucking hell, woman!" He grips my wrist hard until the pressure hurts and causes me to whimper, but a dark, delicious swirl nudges me.

I like it.

"You want to know? You really want to know that my old man would put his smokes out on me? Sometimes, he wouldn't even smoke them. He'd light them, put them out, light them again, only to do it over and over until nothing but the filter was left. And then he'd start all over."

"Logan…" I reach for him while a tear escapes my eye, but he keeps me pinned.

"You want to hear how my mother and I would get beat to

within an inch of our lives, and sometimes my old man would rape her right in front of me. Is that what you want to hear? Or, no, how about this?" He smiles, but it isn't one of happiness, but complete fury. "How about the day I killed him?"

He killed his own father?

"Oh, yeah, little sparrow. I took this same screwdriver—" Tool grabs it from the nightstand and twirls it in his hand. "Well, wait, let me start from the beginning. I came home to him beating my mom, and he was about to rape her again, so I attacked. He reached for this." He waves the screwdriver in the air, making sure he's really making a show of it. "I got to it first. So you know what I did? I drove it between his eyes, right through his skull, and I killed the worthless fuck. I'm good at killing fathers, Juliette. Don't be surprised when I kill yours." He rolls off me and hurries into the bathroom, slamming the door and leaving me alone.

"Oh my god." My voice is shaky and unstable as my brain starts to finally get with the program. Tears sting my cheeks as they freely fall, and I look around for my clothes. My entire body is cold and shaking. I don't know what to think.

I thought he was just a damn weirdo carrying that screwdriver around, but there's an entire story behind it, and now I know why people call him Tool. He uses it to kill.

When I kill your father.

Not if, but when.

At the end of the day, my dad is still my dad, the only one I'll ever have. He can't kill him! I know my dad hasn't been the best man lately, but that doesn't mean he's a bad guy. Everyone makes mistakes, and while I don't want to talk to my dad, I don't want to see him dead either.

The shower turns on, and I take that as Logan's not coming out here to talk to me again. It's good I know the truth, but I shouldn't have pushed. He was right; I wasn't ready. And If I think about it, I'm not mad that he killed his own father. He was an abusive asshole. But my dad? My dad has never hit me besides that one time.

That's all it takes. He'll do it again.

I ignore that pesky little voice in the back of my head while I get dressed. That's when I see my reflection in the mirror. I'm sliding on my panties when I see fingerprint size bruises all over my body. A few red marks from that screwdriver that he dragged down my body. I loved it—the edge of pain. My nipples are swollen and red from how much he sucked on them. There are hickies everywhere—my neck, thighs, and even my ass.

He did hurt me, in really great pleasurable ways, but the hurt he inflicted this morning is something that will take much longer to heal. Once I'm dressed, I push my feet into the red heels and at the last minute, I grab his shirt.

"Come, Tyrant," I call for the dog who's still sleeping in the corner, but once he hears his name he's up and ready to go, unlike Yeti. I fling the door open and run down the hall, only to meet a room full of bikers and women half-dressed. I gulp when everyone stares at me, and Tyrant runs up to a beautiful poodle and starts humping her.

"Like mother like son, am I right?" one of the women says as she openly chews her gum, smacking it. "You're just another bitch, just like this poodle."

"Tyrant, get off. Bad dog, get off," but Tyrant ignores me, humping away like a maniac. Shit, this is so embarrassing.

"He might have fucked you last night, but he won't be fucking you tonight, bitch," a blonde bimbo with fake tits says.

I roll my eyes and yank Tyrant off the poodle. "If I were you, I'd watch what you say, or I'll put you on your back, you know, the place you belong." I sneer at her, and she tries to reach for my neck but another woman grabs her by the hair and shoves her aside.

"Shut up, Candy. You know, Juliette is right. And Tool has never fucked any of you, so stop being jealous bitches." The woman turns to me and grins, but she doesn't introduce herself. She has long hair, olive skin, and bright blue eyes.

"Thanks," I tell her, doing my best to keep my dog by the collar as he tries to hump the poodle again.

"No problem," she says, nodding at a guy with ninja stars in his hand, and they disappear into the back. She doesn't seem like a club whore, but maybe I'm wrong. At least she isn't a bitch.

"Aw, man you should have let him keep going. Poodle would have flipped," he slurs as he narrows his drunken gaze at me. He looks familiar, and as he pulls the bottle of rum up and takes a heavy swig, I realize he's Pirate, the guy from the gate who scared me and ran me off. Yeah. He still scares me. A lot.

I lick my lips at the odd statement and decide I want to get out of here right now. I take a step toward the front door. My palms sweat, and my heart races. I don't like how Pirate is looking at me. I don't like how anyone is looking at me. Panic knots in my chest, tangling like a net and strangling my ability to breathe.

"You have a really pretty tongue," a guy drawls from the couch, sharping a long knife as he stares at my mouth. "Really pretty."

The knot tightens.

"Okay, Tongue. Calm down. Let's go meditate," a woman wearing a 'Property of Reaper' vest helps the guy up. "Look at me, not her, Tongue."

"But—"

"No buts, Tongue. We talked about this," the girl drags him to the back, and I can't help but wonder if meditation means.

I hurry toward the front door, and a man with a black eye stops me. He looks familiar, but I can't place him. His vest says Badge, whatever the hell that name means. "You're going to leave without telling him why?"

I grab the door handle and tears threaten again, but I won't cry in front of everyone. I won't show weakness. "He knows why." I rip the door open and run down the steps, Tyrant hot on my heels. I'm already sweating when the sun hits me because it's so hot.

The sky is bright and cloudless, and heat waves roll over the top of my car from the sun bouncing off the metal. It hurts so bad to leave Logan like this, but I can't be with a man who wants to kill my father. I have to warn him!

Don't I?

Opening the driver's side door, Tyrant gets in and then I follow, not bothering to put on my seatbelt because I need to get the hell out of here. As I reverse and twist the wheel, making the car do a quick 180, I send gravel and dirt everywhere and then speed down the driveway, uncaring of the potholes. I just want to get home and lock my doors, climb under my blanket, and pretend the outside world doesn't exist.

I need to tell my father, but then why is my gut telling me not to? I know if I don't, there's a good chance my father will end up dead. I never asked Tool what my dad had gotten himself into that's so shady because I was still upset about Dad hitting me.

I still am, but is that enough to say he deserves to die? No.

Just what shady shit is he involved in?

"Tyrant, what do I do?" I'm obligated by blood, by the fact that he raised me and gave me everything I needed to tell him, but still, that voice in the back of my head is telling me whatever shit my father is involved in is bad.

"God! Why is this so hard!" It shouldn't be hard. My loyalty needs to be with my dad, not a guy who is half-way to the edge of crazy.

Then why is my heart telling me to not say anything?

The lonely road becomes less lonely real quick when I pass the strip and start heading into the city. Tears are still burning my cheeks, and I can't seem to shut them off. How does the best night of my life turn into the hardest day of my life? I love Logan. I've fallen stupidly in love with him, and I can't stand it.

I hate it.

I love him.

I hate that I love him.

He isn't good for me.

He's the best for me.

I let out a scream of frustration and put my Honda in park with so much anger, I think I broke the gear shifter. I open my driver's side door and jump out, then the door closes from a gust of wind, hitting me in the arm, and I shove it back. I shove it too hard because it hits me again, and a bitter laugh bubbles in my throat. "Tyrant! Let's go."

He jumps out of the car and darts around the front, and in one leap he jumps on the porch and waits by the door. While I'm making my way down the sidewalk, I talk to myself and run through the conversation Logan and I had. "How dare he? He can't threaten me like that," I scoff and slide the key into the lock, twisting it open. "The nerve. Freaking bikers," I grumble and kick my heels off when I step inside and lock the door behind me.

"Don't fucking move," a gravel-filled voice says from behind me, placing a gun against my temple.

Tyrant launches himself at the intruder, and then a gunshot rings out followed by a yelp. I turn around and see my dog laying on the floor, blood coating his fur. "No!" I scream. "Tyrant," I cry when I see him lying there still. I don't know if I'm stupid and have a death wish, or what, but I launch myself at the attacker next. I step on his foot, and he grunts.

"You fucking bitch," he snarls and wraps an arm around my chest.

I bring my elbow back as hard as I can and hit him in the ribs. I pull out of his hold to turn around and lift my knee to hit his balls. He doubles over, and right as I spin on my foot to run to my bedroom to get my gun, because for some stupid reason, I didn't put it in my purse this morning, another guy comes out of the shadows and slams something against my head.

And the last thing I scream for inside my mind before darkness takes over?

Logan!

As if he can hear me through the unconsciousness.

I help Reaper set up the party tent to give us some shade for this heat. The cookout will start a few hours before sundown, and we want to make sure we don't die of a heatstroke. I'm sweating my ass off, thinking that I may just die of a heatstroke, but I'll push through because it's helping me keep my mind off Juliette and the life-changing night we spent together. She left, just like I gave her the option to. I hoped she wouldn't have, but it wasn't like she could read my mind.

She did what I wanted her to do, and now she can be free of me and my fucking poison.

"You okay?" Reaper asks, stabbing the stand with the white pole, sending up a cloud of dust.

"Fine," I grunt, pulling the material of the tent over the rods to make sure it's secure.

"Liar. Talk to me."

"You asking as a friend or my Prez?" I'm ashamed that I wear his warning mark, and I'm happy as hell he hasn't asked about it. As a friend, I'm sure he wants to. As the Prez? He doesn't fucking care.

Lines can get blurred if someone isn't smart, but luckily, Reaper is the smartest around this place.

"Both. What happened with Juliette?"

I take the screwdriver out from behind my ear and tighten a bolt that connects two of the rods. Huh, that's the first time I've used this damn thing for what it's supposed to be used for. "I told her my truths, and she didn't like it. End of story."

"Truths sometimes take a minute to wrap your head around. She'll be back."

"Should have never told her. A lie of omission is better than the truth."

"A lie is a lie no matter how you word it, Tool. You didn't lie to her about what made you who you are, and you didn't lie to her about what you do. It's up to her now. Give her time. This life isn't easy."

"A lie is easier than the truth," I say, shorter and curter than I mean to sound, but I'm grumpy as hell without Juliette at my side. I knew that someone as good as her wouldn't want someone like me. My dad was right about one thing—no one needs to be stuck with me.

She's free of me.

"Of course it's easier," he laughs. "Anything worth it is never easy, Tool."

I want to talk about something else, anything else, but my lack of ability to properly fucking love someone. "How many chapters are coming today?" I finally get the last pole in the ground and want to collapse when the big fucker is finally standing. It took hours. I'm sweating so much; my shirt is glued to my skin.

"All of them." Reaper sits on a mound of dirt and opens a red cooler that's filthy with grime and age. It's a nineties cooler, one that doesn't keep the ice very long and you have to press buttons on either side of the handle to lift it. Throwback. He can afford a better one. I don't know why he keeps that piece of shit. "Want one?"

"Fuck yeah." An ice-cold beer sounds perfect. "All of them, really? That's impressive."

"When the original chapter invites you to a cookout, you don't say no; you get me?" We pop the top to our Bud Lights, which tastes like watered down piss, which he knows, but on a day like this, it tastes like the heaven between Juliette's legs as it slides down my throat.

"I'm not familiar with a lot of them," I admit, thinking back to the Boston chapter. "I only know of the Boston chapter when ... yeah, when they got me and my mom out of there."

"They will be here."

"No, shit?" Maybe I'll actually get to see my mom for the first time in a few years. Brass, the President of the Boston chapter declared his love for her, and I didn't think she'd ever go back to that city, but she hopped on that bike with him and left, and she's she been his ol' lady ever since.

"Yeah, your mom should be coming, along with the New Orleans, Miami, Detroit, Seattle, Chicago, Memphis, and Nashville chapters. Boomer's club might roll in too."

"No shit? Boomer? Really?" I hope the guy comes. He and Sarah have shit they need to clear up, and I know Reaper wants to see him. "That's a lot of fucking hogs. The desert is going to be full." I'm pumped. It's exactly what I need to get my mind off Juliette. Just a bunch of my MC brothers, shooting the shit, and who fucking knows what trouble we'll get into tonight. We have one hundred acres of desert to fuck with, and a lot can happen when the Ruthless Kings get together and night strikes.

A roar of motorcycles sound in the distance, and Reaper grins. "Ah, looks like the fuckers are starting to arrive." We look toward the road when Skirt's ass greets us. "Fuck, Skirt, put that shit away."

"I'm just getting me a drink, Prez."

"Cover your ass while you do it," Reaper mumbles and takes a swig of his beer then rubs the cold condensation from his fingers over his sweaty face.

"You like me arse; don't play like ye don't." Skirt walks over to Poodle who is currently yelling at my dog because Yeti is trying to get it on with Lady. I told Poodle I wasn't going to stop my boy from getting it in, and I meant it. I want to piss off Poodle naturally.

"That damn guy, he's going to kill me with a heart attack one day when he flashes his ass. I don't understand why he won't wear underwear." Reaper stands and holds out his hand to help me get up. "Let's go introduce our guests to everyone."

I slap my hand in his and stand, watching one by one as the bikes come to a stop in front of the clubhouse. There's about ten of them, and I'm sure some guys stayed behind to watch their clubhouses like usual.

As I stand and watch one by one as my MC brothers pull up, I think about Juliette. She's never far from my mind, and I wanted her to be here tonight, to get a sense of how things really are, but I had to go and let my fear get the best of me.

People don't know this, but I'm fucking scared all the time, and it's what drives me to do what I do for Reaper, for the club. Taking a life isn't easy, but every time I drive that screwdriver between someone's eyes, I'm reminded of the peace I felt when my father took his last breath, and fear leaves me.

Until the next time.

The rest of the Vegas members crowd behind us, taking a break from setting up seats and tables for food. I whistle when I see the lead bike, who must be the Prez, pull in. It has black-on-black everything with wide-set handles and a long front end. I squint my eyes when I see carvings along the metal of his bike.

Voodoo heads.

That isn't fucking weird or unsettling.

Still, it's a sweet ride.

"Voodoo," Reaper greets with the biggest damn smile I've seen from him in a few days. "It's good to see you. Been too damn long."

"Mon Ami." The man pulls Reaper into a quick hug, patting him on the back in a few hard slaps. He has a thick Cajun accent and a scar around his neck, like he was strangled with a wire or something similar. "It's been too damn long; you're right. 'Bout time you got your head out of your ass and threw a party."

"Shit has been busy in Vegas. I actually might need you and some of your guys to stick around for a few extra days. I'll explain why later."

"Fuck, it's hot," a guy as big as me stands next to Voodoo, and when I glance at the patch, it says VP, like me. "My balls are sticking to my leg."

Voodoo snorts and tilts his head in his VP's direction. "This is my right-hand man, Caster."

"Tool," I hold out my hand, and Caster meets it, then narrows his eyes as he tugs me close. "I'm uh … Reaper's VP."

"Don't mind Caster. He has a way of reading people," Voodoo tries to settle my nerves, but it doesn't work.

The man has long dreads, mixed skin, and bright blue eyes that almost look white, which creep me the fuck out. "You have demons inside you, Tool." He cocks his head, gripping my hand tighter.

"What the fuck?" I growl, not liking another testing me. I try

188

to pull my hand away, but Caster keeps a tight hold, analyzing me.

"You are a good killer." His eyes come to the screwdriver tucked in between my ear like it always is. "You are haunted by that weapon. Too much darkness lingers."

"What the hell is he talking about?" I ask, getting a bit freaked out with this psycho-babble bullshit. "Reaper, what did you tell him?"

"Not shit, Tool. I swear," Reaper says.

"I'm gonna piss myself if this shit continues." Skirt's Scottish accent invades the tense moment, and I want to laugh.

"Me too," Poodle joins in.

They want to piss themselves. What about me? I have a crazy person staring at me.

"Ya know New Orleans has a lot of superstition, yes?" Voodoo asks me and I nod, knowing it's just myths and tourist grabbing bullshit when people go to visit. "Caster has a long history with an interesting background. If he's talking to you, mon ami, you better listen. He hasn't been wrong yet."

"Let go of me," I threaten as he squeezes my hand harder. I can't kick this guy's ass because a fight will not be good at maintaining peace, but this guy is crossing a line.

"Someone you love is in danger. A lot of danger."

I snort. "If that isn't the most cliché thing I've ever heard." I look around at my brothers' faces to see how they're reacting, and a few of them are eating this shit up like it's a movie. A few are skeptical, like my man Tongue, being all weird and brooding in the back. His arms are crossed, and he narrows his eyes at Caster in disbelief.

"Two women." And on that fucking note, he lets go of my hand.

"What the hell do you mean two women?" My heart thuds against my chest with panic. I grab his arm, and his eyes laser into me again.

"Now you want to know more?"

"Go easy on him, Caster. This is supposed to be a good time," Voodoo says from beside him. Another roar of motorcycles come, and this time when they enter the parking lot there are a few more chapters with them. It looks like Memphis and Nashville.

"Please, when you say two women, who are you talking about?" There are only two women in my life who mean anything to me. "Caster, please. Whatever weird shit you're capable of, I need you to tell me."

"Your demons have followed you from a long way, mon ami," he says, patting my hand. Another roar interrupts us, but this time, the bikes sound different; they sound manic and quick as they zip down the drive.

The bikes come into view and I see the first cut, and I notice it's the Boston chapter. Something's wrong.

"Two women you love. I cannot see faces. One has long brown hair and the other—"

Brass' bike crashes to the ground because he doesn't bother putting it on its stand. He runs over to us, his VP and Sargent at

Arms on his heels.

"The other is older. A tattoo on her inner wrist of your name?"

I let go of Caster's hand and stumble back, staring at him with disbelief. "That's my mom," I whisper. "The other sounds like Juliette." How can I take his word for it? I'm just supposed to accept with wide open arms that this guy from New Orleans has some witch fucking voodoo. I don't believe in that kind of shit.

"Reaper! Tool! Tool? Where's Tool?" Brass shouts, and everyone turns to him, and he's red faced and panicked.

"Brass? What the hell is going on?" Reaper cuts through the crowd.

Brass falls to his knees and spreads his arms, clenching his hands in tight fists, roaring into the sky his sorrow. "Someone took her. Someone took Whitney."

I push Reaper out of the way and grab Brass, the President of the Boston chapter, and sling him to the ground. "What the hell? What are you talking about? Who took her? Who took my fucking mom? Why didn't you protect her?" I lift my fist, and Reaper catches it mid-air.

"That isn't going to help anyone," he says, then turns his eyes to Caster. "Did you see anything else? Or felt … or whatever you do."

"No," he says simply, not describing more or less of what he can do.

"Where is she?" I scream at him and try to tackle Brass again, but Tongue is there along Reaper's side.

191

"I'll cut your tongue out if you have anything to do with this," Tongue points his knife at Brass in warning.

"If anything happens to her, you can kill me. I love Whitney—"

"Something has happened to her! It has to be the sheriff. He has to be behind this!" I yell at him, and my head pounds from the amount of force it takes to push my voice to its limit. This can't be happening again. She's supposed to be safe. I made sure of it. She was safe. With Brass. Dad is dead. He can't hurt her anymore.

Juliette. Where is she? I need to go. I need to make sure she's at home. She has to be. Caster Crazy Eyes is a fucking liar. He's a fake. None of that shit is real. New Orleans bullshit can go back to where it came from.

"I need you to take a deep breath and calm the hell down if you want to figure this out," Reaper says in a calm, steady tone. "Brass, what happened?"

Brass, the sad man who dares call himself the President and my mother's protector, shakes his head as if he's in denial. "We were at the hotel. Nothing out of the ordinary. If I would have known that your club was in trouble, I never would have let her go to the damn vending machine alone. I didn't know. I swear to god, I wouldn't have let her go alone."

He should have been with her anyway. That makes me a hypocrite. I'm not with Juliette, and I hate myself for it. Women of the club, women of the members are always strong, and we can't always have someone with them because our girls would've found a way to do something alone anyway, unknowingly putting themselves in danger.

We should have called this damn cookout off, or at the very least we should've told everyone about the threat in Vegas right now.

I take my screwdriver and fling it right by Brass' head. It lands in the sand with a hard thud, making sand fly in his eyes. I don't give a fuck if the bastard goes blind, not after he didn't protect my mom. "The next time I throw it, you won't be so lucky," I say, pulling out of Reaper and Tongue's arms. "I'm fine." They try grabbing me again, and I take a step back. "I said I'm fucking fine!" I tug my weapon from the ground and debate if I want to kill Brass now. "I trusted you to keep her safe. If I would have known that you couldn't, I would have made her stay with me."

"I know. I know. I'm sorry, Tool. I'm sorry."

"Sorry doesn't fucking do anything, does it?" I lift my arm to put the asshole out of his misery, out of my misery, and Tongue stops me, catching my arm as I bring it down. The screwdriver stops just as the tip hits between Brass' eyes, digging into his skin. Blood flows over his nose and down his cheek, but it isn't enough. I want more.

I need more.

Another grumble of motorcycles comes, and I don't care who it is.

I'm surrounded by an army of bikers, but I've never felt more on my own in my entire life.

I push Tongue away and run toward my bike. I need to check

on Juliette. I need to make sure she's okay. Caster is wrong. He's full of crap and it's only coincidence. That's all.

"Tool!" Reaper shouts after me, but I don't stop. I can't afford to stop. All I see is my mom needing help, and this time I can do more than I could when I was fifteen. I hop on my hog, and Tongue is right beside me.

He gives me a quick nod, and then Caster is getting on his bike too. "No, you can stay."

"Ya need me. I can see more than ya can."

"I don't give a fuck if you can see into goddamn space—you aren't fucking coming!" I crank my bike, and the engine grumbles between my legs, adding to the group of motorcycles coming down the driveway. Looks like the rest of the chapters showed up.

When I reverse, I'm careful to miss a few custom-made bikes and see Badge getting on his bike too. I don't bother to see where he's going. The only thing on my mind is my mom and Juliette. How can this be happening to me? What does someone want with me?

I hit the throttle, and my back tire spins against the dirt, flinging gravel. I hear it hit metal, and I know I'm denting bikes, but again, I don't care. I need out of here. Speeding down the driveway, I pass the Chicago, Detroit, and Miami chapter.

I don't wave. I don't acknowledge them. I just get the hell out of dodge as if the devil is nipping at my back tire. When the road comes to view, I turn my handlebars sharp to the right and almost run into a car. They blare their horn at me, and I swerve to miss the front of the Chevy Cruise and my foot hits the fender, but I don't stop. I'll break every bone in my body in attempt to save the only women who matter to me.

I'll give my life if it means getting theirs back.

I twist the throttle, opening my bike on the open road with Juliette's house in mind. Everything disappears as my vision tunnels. The wind dries my eyes and stings my cheeks. My hair is blowing all over the place, and I think about the worst-case scenario when I get to Juliette's. It has me almost losing control and going off the side of the road when I imagine finding her body, dead, and I'll never get to hear her beautiful voice again.

Or experience the goodness of her.

I take a right down her street, noticing the sign in the ground saying to 'Vote' with a checkmark next to the word is laying on the ground and fresh tire tracks imprinted in the red clay of the ground. I know that whatever it is, those tracks have everything to do with Juliette. Once I see her house, I take a note out of Brass' book and don't even bother putting my bike on its stand. The tires have barely stopped rolling when I jump off my seat and then hop over the small fence.

A grumble of motorcycles has me looking back, and damn, my entire MC came out it looks like.

Even the rest of the chapters. It's an overwhelming amount of support, and they have taken over the entire road. Tongue, Caster, and Reaper run down the walkway until they're at my side. Reaper slaps me on the shoulder, and Tongue tugs his knife out of his cut.

"Ya won't need that here," Caster says as his white eyes dart around the house, reading it. "There are no threats here, mon ami."

I take that as a good sign. If there are no threats, then that must mean Juliette is safe. She's singing, dancing in the kitchen and happy. She has to be.

Please, let her be.

I run up the steps and notice the door cracked open. "No," I whisper simply as I push it open and stand in the middle of the doorway. No one needs to tell me what happened. I can feel it. She isn't here. That fucking psycho-babble bullshit from Caster was right. I turn on my heel, grab the fucker by his cut, and drag him up the stairs, throwing him in the house. "What happened! Tell me."

"You believe me now?" He lifts a thick brow with a large hoop piercing it.

"No, I don't know. I'm just willing to believe anything, to do anything." I look down at my boots to see blood, and I fall to my knees. "No, no, no," I roar and stab the floor with the screwdriver.

"That is not her blood." Caster takes two steps to the right and squats, sliding his fingers through the pool of sanguine liquid.

"Enough of this," I stomp my way through the house, my boots matching the heavy pound of my heart, and when I get to her bedroom door, I hear I high-pitched whine. I step through, waiting to see a nightmare. "Tyrant!" I run to the side of the bed when I notice her dog lying next to it, breathing quickly, when I see his lungs rise and fall so fast. He's shot. I scoop him up in my arms, and he whines again. "I got you, buddy. It's okay. Just hold on a little longer, okay? Hold on for me." I hold him to my chest and run down the hall. Caster doesn't look surprised, but he couldn't have known about this. He's too much. I can't deal with Caster anymore and to be honest, he's too supernatural for my blood. Whatever shit he has going on, I don't want it around me. I can't have it around me.

"Mon ami," Caster speaks to Tyrant in his Cajun accent and touches the dog's head. Tyrant instantly calms. "Oh, you've seen a lot, haven't you?"

"Enough," I snap. "I don't know what kind of whisperer you are, dog, human, fucking alien; just stay away from me." Reaper takes Tyrant from my arms, and when I look down, I have blood on my cut. For the first time, it isn't human.

"I'll take him to the vet. You do what you have to do." A lot of the guys leave when Reaper does, but Tongue stays and so does Caster. I guess he can't take a fucking hint.

"Where are they?" I ask, looking around the room for any clues, for anything they left behind. Whoever is behind this, I'm going to kill them. I'm going to drive my tool so far into their skull many times until their brain is leaking out of every wound. I focus on the hate inside me, letting it possess me, and the urge to kill is so strong I can nearly taste it on my tongue.

No one fucks with what is mine.

I'll save my mom. I'll save my girl.

And then I'll kill anyone who looks my way.

Hate is a powerful emotion, especially when it's derived out of love.

I groan when I finally wake up. My head is throbbing, and I feel like I have a bad case of motion sickness with how my stomach is turning like everything is swaying, or maybe I'm swaying. Either way, I'm about to vomit. I close my eyes again and take deep breaths. In through my nose and out through my mouth.

"Hey, girl. Wake up. Hey!" Someone's foot kicks mine and when I open my eyes again, I see an older woman with black hair and dark eyes. Her skin is a bit wrinkled, but she looks like someone I know. "Hey, how are you feeling? Are you okay?" the woman asks, hands tied behind her back, and her ankles are strapped together too.

Like mine.

"I'm … confused," I finally find the right words. "Where are we? Who are you?"

"I'm Whitney. I'm Logan's mom."

I gasp in terror when I see she has a black eye and a busted lip. That's why she looks so familiar. Her and Logan share a lot of the same features. "I wish I could say it was good to meet you, but I didn't want to meet you like this. I'm Juliette, Logan's... I don't know."

"Logan's girlfriend. I know my son. He doesn't get involved, so if he's involved with you, that means something."

I shake my head when I remember that last thing he said to me. I know I don't mean a damn thing to him. "Do you know where we are?" it looks like jail cells, but older, and it's dark from the lack of windows.

"I don't know," she says, tugging on the restraints until her skin breaks. "We aren't the only women here, though, but we were taken intentionally because of Logan."

"How do you know that?" My lip starts to tremble, and that's when I know I'm about to freak out. I can't do that. I'm trained for this. My dad trained me to get out of situations like this. I'll be fine.

"Because I noticed the man who took me. I haven't seen him in a long time, and I have no idea what he's doing here, but it's him. I don't doubt it."

"Who?"

"At the time he was just a prospect for the MC. He helped dispose of..."

"Logan's dad's body? Yeah, he told me." I hit my head against the wall, and a cold breeze comes through the cracks in the cement foundation, and I shiver.

"Well, it's him and my damn dead's husband stepbrother. I'm not too sure what the hell they want with Logan, but it's some serious shit. I'm worried for my boy. He's strong, but he has carried revenge in his heart for an awfully long time. If he never finds us, he will blame himself."

"He'll find us. My dad will find us. He's the—" A door opens in the distance, and the clink of metal reverberates around us as voices get closer. "That's him. That's—" I feel hope swell in my chest when I hear my dad's voice. "Dad! Dad! Help us! We're over here," I shout with relieved tears pouring down my face.

"Your dad is the sheriff?"

"Yeah." I nod enthusiastically, knowing we are about to get out of here.

"Juliette, I hate to tell you this—" Whitney is interrupted when my dad stands in front of the jail cell with another guy who has a scar down the left side of his face. He's staring at me with hunger as he licks his lips and grabs his crotch.

My dad wraps his hands around the bars and leans in, allowing the hallway light to shine on his face. It's the same dark look he gave me when I moved out. "Dad? What's going on? Let us out." I tug on the cuffs, but it's no use. They aren't going anywhere. I'm sitting on an old stained cot on one side of the room, and Whitney is on the other cot.

Dad groans in frustration. "Stop calling me that. God, I've waited so long to say that. Raising your ass was fucking exhausting."

I almost don't understand the words coming from his mouth. They hurt too much. "What are you talking about?"

"You. You were just some crack baby that a whore I fucked had. I wanted nothing to do with you, but then she came up with an amazing idea. We would raise you and at the right age, sell you."

My mouth drops open, and I barely get to the edge of the bed before I puke. "No!" I shake my head with denial, and Whitney pulls against her cuffs to try to get to me, staring at me with pity.

"Leave her alone," Whitney barks, and my dad gives her a look that could kill.

"She deserves the truth. Listen, pumpkin," he laughs at the nickname he has called me for the last twenty-five years. "You were never even supposed to be born. I promised a guy that he could have you for the right price on the stipulation that you had to remain a virgin, but you didn't fucking do that. You had to go and be a damn whore, pumpkin. What did I tell you about doing that? What did I tell you about whores?"

I turn my face into the wall and cry, my heart shattering until I feel like I can't breathe or think. My entire life was a lie just to prepare me for my dad to get a big payday.

"That fucking biker ruined everything, and that's when I knew I had to make my move. And you know what's even sweeter, pumpkin? That bastard's father was my stepbrother. Logan deserves this for driving a screwdriver through my brother's head." The man who used to be my father grabs a pack of cigarettes out of his pocket and puts a long white smoke between his lips. "It's poetic, kind of, right? That we have the bitch who wasn't a good wife, the bastard son who loves my daughter, but he isn't allowed to."

"What do you want?" I ask, not really caring what he has to say. It doesn't matter.

"What do I want? I want to fucking ruin Logan's life like he ruined mine. Luckily, Ziggy here was willing to give me all the information I needed to set Logan up. We all go way back, ya see, so I promised him the payday once we sold you, and then he could do the honors of killing Logan. To think I almost did this right before Logan happened, but then I started to think smart." He taps the side of his head. "I can't believe how good this worked out. It's like it was meant to be or something."

"Why wait until now?" I ask him, tasting tears on my lips as I cry.

"I wanted to wait until I had the means to do what I needed to do. I had a few people lined up to set Logan up for murder along with this little operation we have going on here. Since you fucked him, I can't sell you. That's what happens when I wait too long, but I can make money off you. We have a few fights tonight, pumpkin, and the winners will get to fuck you. Hell the losers can too as long as they pay. I really don't give a fuck."

"I want to go first," the guy next to the man who shaped my future to be a nightmare growls.

"Then fight," the sheriff says, slapping his friend in the chest.

"Don't do this," I beg. "It doesn't have to be like this."

203

"It does, though, because I'm tired of you. I'm tired of the Ruthless Kings thinking they can get away with whatever they want. I'm tired of my stepbrother's killer walking around as if he's allowed to be. It took a long time to become Sheriff, but now I can be untouchable. I can get away with anything I want, and the first thing on my list is Logan."

"Doesn't make sense." Whitney rolls her head back and forth, trying to understand the crazy man's logic. "If you hated him so much, why not just take him out and do whatever you wanted with Juliette?"

"Because," he says darkly, lowering his voice, and the evil trembles wrap around me. I can hear the smile in his voice as he continues. He blows out a puff of smoke first, "Because revenge is sweeter when the execution plan is detailed. It was sheer dumb luck that Juliette and Logan found each other. Ah, love, it's a stupid fucking thing, isn't it? Well, lay back, ladies. Get comfortable."

"All those times," I whisper, squeezing my eyes shut when I think about all the birthday parties, presents, kisses on the forehead. All of the moments he showed me love, it was fake. "All the times we spent together; you really didn't care about me. You're okay with your daughter getting used for your own gain? What kind of Sheriff does that make you? What kind of father?" I spit, yanking with all my might against the cuffs in hopes I can launch myself at his disgusting, lying face.

"Pumpkin, I only ever cared to be one of those things." He flicks the cigarette at me, and it's still hot, glowing red at the end. It hits against my stomach, burning a hole in my shirt until it singes my skin. I cry out and roll out of the way, then kick it off the bed until it falls into a puddle on the floor, extinguishing instantly. "Come on, Zig. Money is waiting." My dad—not my captor—turns around with an evil twist to his face, a face only the devil can love, and walks away.

His friend turns to me and leans his head between the bars. "I'll be seeing you later, Juliette." His laughter is menacing, a true villain wanting to ruin the fairy tale I have planned for my life. Their footsteps get farther away until the door slams shut, locking us inside what damnation must look like.

"Logan will come for us," Whitney says. "I know he will. I'm sorry about your father. That entire family was terrible when I was married to Logan's father. I'm thankful Logan killed him, or I would have been used for the rest of my life. I never thought that day would come back and haunt me with a vengeance. The prospect then, Ziggy, if I remember correctly, was with Brass that night. Ziggy was a backstabber then, and the club kicked him out. It makes sense that his stepbrother found out what really happened. I bet Zig told Derek about his brother's death out of retaliation for the club kicking him out. You were just a little girl at the time..." Realization dawns on her face. "oh my god." Whitney closes her eyes, and a tear rolls down her cheek. "I remember you. I met you once when you were just a little girl. That bastard came over, and Logan watched you when... It doesn't matter. But you guys have been a part of each other's lives a lot longer than you think."

"We … aren't related, are we?"

She snorts. "No, your dad is just my ex's stepbrother."

"Oh, good. That's good. That would have been awkward if I ever saw him again." If I ever see him again.

"You'll see him. We will get out of this."

"How do you know?" I ask, losing hope with every word I have to speak.

"Because I've seen Logan protect the people he loves. He will go to every extreme to protect the people he loves."

Will it be too late, though? Will we get used up and tossed aside with our lips stitched shut? Will Logan will be pinned for murder?

I only want to see Logan's face again and tell him I don't care that he killed his dad.

And I don't care that he has to kill mine.

Have fucking at it. Just let me be in his arms again.

I've been to her dad's house, and there's nothing there that tells me where he is. He isn't at the police station. No one has seen him since yesterday. I'm on the verge of completely losing it. I don't care if the person is innocent or not. If they get in my way, I don't think I'll be able to stop myself.

I'll kill them along with everyone else who took my little sparrow. I'll save her and make sure her wings are never clipped again. Juliette will only ever know freedom when I have her again.

Right now, I'm in the basement, interrogating a gang member who is very familiar with that house I saw the sheriff at a few nights ago. "Tell me what I want to know," I say, flexing my fingers to release the ache. I've punched for a few hours and have maintained a tight grip around my screwdriver.

"I ain't telling you shit." The guy wheezes but gives me a cocky smile that I want to annihilate from his face.

I've been going at him for about an hour, but he won't say shit about that house. I rip my screwdriver from his thigh and plunge it in his gut next, twisting and turning so the metal wraps around all of his organs. He screams until he nearly passes out, and that's when I pull out the weapon. He tries to take a deep breath. "Is that so? Alright, then. Tongue? Do your worst," I tell my MC brother, and he steps from the shadows with a glint of excitement in his eyes.

"Wait, what's he do? Who is that?"

"He's going to make sure you never speak again." I wipe my hands on a rag and notice how ruined and fucked up my knuckles are. His face is worse; that much I can say. His eyes are swollen, cheeks are busted, and his lip is bleeding. Even Knives got in a few hits with his Ninja Star, and the guy still won't talk.

"What's that mean?" The guy shakes, his naked body trembling when Tongue takes a step closer. I have to say, I'd be freaking the fuck out too if Tongue walked close to me with a knife, planning to slice out my own tongue.

Tongue grips the guy's chin, tilts his head back, and brings his face down until Tongue is almost kissing him, turning his head left and right. It's almost like he's debating on turning this into something dirtier. He bumps the guy's nose and grins, then brings his mouth to his ear. "I'm going to slice your tongue out and feed it to the coyotes," Tongue says in his typical slow drawl. The tip of the knife hits under the guy's chin, and Tongue runs the sharp edge down his chest. He cuts a shallow wound on the man's skin that goes from his chin to the middle of his chest. "And if you don't drown from swallowing your own blood, my friend Bullseye is going to play darts with your heart. And then my Prez is going to reach in"— Tongue licks his lips as he swirls the knife over the guy's nipples—"and take your beating heart from your chest."

The smell of piss fills the air, and our captive shakes his head. "I'll tell you. Fuck, I'll tell you what I know. I swear to god, don't cut my tongue out."

"But I want to," Tongue pouts.

"Tongue," I say his name with an extra bite, telling him to back away. Tongue sighs, then takes a step back.

"I never get to have any fun." And like a toddler, he leans back and crosses his arms over his chest.

"Talk," I say.

"The house is where a lot of the fights happen. People off the street looking for an extra buck or high go there. Tonight, there's a special prize for the winners. They have girls there willing to fuck, but I swear to god that's all I know. I swear." The man pisses again, and the drain gurgles as it sucks in the dehydrated body fluid.

That's pretty good information. "Why didn't you tell us this earlier?"

"Because my crew goes there all the time. I can't snitch on my crew, man." Spit gathers on the man's chin and drips down on the metal floor. His spit is tinted red with blood, and seeing him beaten and broken has power surging through my veins, strengthening me for what's about to come.

"Tongue, finish him off," I give the order, and Tongue gives me the biggest smile as he pushes off the wall with his boot.

"What do you mean? I—I told you. I told you what you wanted to know. No, man. Don't. Please. Oh, god," the man cries, snot dripping from down from his nose to his lips and chin. It's disgusting.

Tongue wraps a hand around the man's jaw, bringing the knife to his lips and play bites the air, causing the man to jump. I throw the rag on the floor and right as I leave, Tongue says to our captive, "God doesn't live here."

Painful, soul-wrenching screams resound in the devil's playroom, followed by Tongue's wicked, victorious laughter. Blood gurgles as the man chokes and tries to live.

"Someone stich his lips up and deliver his body to the house. I want a message being sent."

"Can I stitch his mouth together with his own tongue?"

"I don't give a fuck how you do it; just do it," I sneer and kick the door open to find Doc standing between the bed Moretti lays in and the young deputy who is barely hanging on. Just a fucking kid. His lips are swollen, blood red dots decorate his top and bottom lips, and his eyes are shut from being so swollen. Doc had to drain the sides of his face from all the blood gathering, and it looks like he might have to do it again.

Sarah is between the beds, rocking in a chair and reading a Harry Potter book aloud. She thinks it helps them heal when they can hear a friendly voice. She even does different voices for all the characters. Reaper always stares at her with love in his eyes as she reads, but I know who she really wants to do this for. A baby. Her baby, but it might not happen, and that's why she's reading to the guys who are hanging on to life.

The young deputy, crybaby, as we call him now, is also in a coma, medically-induced, but Doc thought it was best considering all of his injuries.

"Swish and flick," Sarah reads in a higher pitched voice that's not her own. She sees me and marks the book, closing it softly as if she's afraid to wake either men beside her. "Anything?"

I nod and place my hand on the rail that leads up the stairs. "Yeah, I'm going to go tell Reaper now. He has a clubhouse full of bikers who want an update."

"You'll find her, Tool. You deserve good things, no matter what you think."

"I don't know what you're talking about," I say quietly.

"I've heard you, having nightmares, you know; screaming at the top of your lungs. It always sounds like you're fighting someone. That person isn't around anymore, Tool."

My face burns with shame. I had no idea people heard me.

Sarah opens the book again to start reading, but Reaper bellows from the basement door. "Get up here. Now. Get Tongue and Bullseye too," he shouts before slamming the door shut.

"I'll get them. You go ahead," Sarah says, laying the book on the nightstand and rocks forward to stand.

"Thanks," I reply, needing to get the hell away from her before she tells me any more secrets. As I climb up the steps, I think about how fucking tired I am of living my life in a void, and how Juliette is the only one who's been able to pull me from its darkness.

I open the door, but I don't bother going to the main room because it isn't big enough to hold a hundred plus bikers. The auditorium is a huge basketball court, and Reaper had a pool installed too for Sarah because she loves to swim. I pass through the kitchen and dining room and open the door to another hallway. It's nothing special. The hallway itself is pretty plain and still smells of fresh paint.

The plain industrial doors that one finds in a school comes to view, and I push the door open to see a wave of black cuts on the bleachers. A lot of the chapters are staying here, wanting to camp out to be close to base while most of them are staying in a hotel on the strip. I wish my club was done being renovated and all this shit wasn't going on, then we would be having a good time. My girl can be the singer, the main attraction with a voice like hers, and I'll be the lucky sonofabitch who doesn't deserve her but gets to take her home every night.

I rub the ache in my chest, and not the one that Reaper made, but the one that missing someone makes. It's that hollow, helpless feeling, the one that makes the body feel heavy. I'm back in that damn void, and I'm afraid if I don't find Juliette soon, no one will be able to pull me out.

I'll need to inflict pain on people, and I don't want that for myself, but it's the only way to alleviate the edge and anger inside me .

"Tool." Reaper gets off the bottom bleacher and meets me halfway. "We have someone who really wants to help."

"Reaper, listen, Caster and that entire New Orleans chapter are loyal to the fucking bone, but they fucking creep me out. I can't be next to Caster. Don't make me work with him."

"You scared?"

"Of shit I don't understand. Like fucking voodoo witchcraft, psychic reading bullshit? Yeah, Reap. That freaks me the fuck out, and I'm afraid I'll kill Caster with how edgy I feel."

Reaper nods and puts his hand on my shoulder. "That's not who wants to work with us." Reaper steps to the side, and damn if the kid doesn't look grown.

"Boomer," I say in shock. I thought I'd be furious seeing him again, but I'm relieved.

"Hey, Tool." He steps forward, and a few guys flank his sides. He has a patch on his cut that says President, and the guy next to him has a VP patch. His name is Arrow, which makes sense because the fucker is carrying a bow over his shoulder. The next guy is Kansas. I remember him from Jersey, but Arrow not so much. And then there is Wolf, with a patch that says Sargent in Arms. He stayed around. Good. He's good men for an MC to have.

"It's good to see you, man. Have you seen Sarah?" I give him a quick hug then nod toward all the guys. "Nice to see you on your

213

feet. Decide what to name your MC?"

"No, not yet. Still debating if I want to keep it a Ruthless chapter or not. We are rebuilding, so there's no rush. And I haven't seen her yet." He scratches his head, and the big bad President of his new club looks nervous. "She okay? I want to talk to her after we all talk, and you can update me on what's going on. Is it anything like what happened in Jersey?"

I shake my head, trying to connect to see if there are any dots. "No, it's nothing like that. We think there's an underground fight club with a prostitution ring, and that's where they are keeping..." My voice breaks from emotion, and I stop myself from speaking for a second. I can't look like a pussy in front of a hundred badass bikers. "That's where my mom and Juliette are. Go talk to Sarah. Reaper and I need to plan. I think I have the perfect way to get in that house."

"Well, I'm ready to blow shit up whenever you want me to. I'm going to go talk with my sister and hope she doesn't kill me. It's been awhile."

"She misses you." Reaper nudges him. "She needs you. Go on."

Kansas and Arrow stay behind while Wolf walks with him, but Boomer tells Wolf to stay behind. The guy looks absolutely lost since he has to stay back with the rest of us. We watch Boomer's blank cut walk away from us, and it's hard to believe he lives all the way in Jersey now, settled down with an ol'" lady and everything. When the hell did that happen? Crazy.

214

"What's your plan?" Reaper asks me, leading me to the bench where Voodoo and Caster are. I growl low in my throat at Reap. He's making me sit down near them on purpose.

"Well, we can buy our way in a fight. It can be a distraction while a group of guys look for the girls."

"Who's going to fight?" Poodle asks from beside Caster. Lady is laying by his feet alongside Yeti. Hell, I'm glad my dog has found his home with everyone. I've been a shitbag owner for not being around more.

"I can fight," the prospect Tim speaks up, pushing his glasses up his nose as he looks at us with big eyes through thick lenses.

The entire auditorium goes silent, and Tim's large Adam's apple bobs with nerves. He feels all the eyes on him, and it's causing him to squirm.

"Tim, how much do ye weigh? A buck ten, soaking wet? Hell, my left nut is bigger than ye; no offense, lad."

"Really? No offense? You compared me to your nut, Skirt. And I weigh one hundred and fifty pounds," he mutters, shy and timid, but he flexes his muscles anyway to show us his scrawny arms. My pit bull has more muscle than he does.

Jesus Christ, he'll get killed if we put him in a fighting ring.

Reaper rubs a hand over his face, and Tank chuckles quietly behind Tim. "I appreciate your enthusiasm, Tim, but you're a little small—"

"No really, I can fight. I can take down any guy. Swear," he says, puffing out his chest. "Put someone up against me now, and

I'll take them down."

"Your funeral," Reaper replies, clearly not believing Tim and, to be honest, I don't either. "But this I got to see. Voodoo, pick one of your guys."

"Reaper," I hiss his name, wondering what he's doing. "They could cheat using their New Orleans … stuff."

"Thought ya didn't believe in it?" Voodoo grins cheekily, popping a peanut in his mouth. He finds my discomfort amusing, and it isn't funny. Whatever shit they're into really freaks me the hell out.

"I don't," I grumble and take a seat right next to Caster who gives me a knowing grin as he lights up a joint then hands it to me. "No, thanks." I'll probably end up tripping fucking balls with whatever witchy shit he put in that, and I need a clear head. I'm not about to fuck up this plan and risk Juliette's life because I got high.

"Bones!" Voodoo shouts then cackles like a hyena when the biggest motherfucker I've ever seen stands up. He must be nearing seven feet with muscles the size of boulders. One of his arms must weigh the same as Tim, but when I take a glance at Tim, he doesn't seem the least bit worried.

Bones shakes the entire auditorium as he stomps down the bleachers, like a fucking giant. His ears have gages with these white iron looking horns through them. His cut looks like a damn crop top women wear. I have a feeling they don't make his size.

"You sure about this, Braveheart?" Bones' voice is so deep,

and I can hardly understand him, but his nickname for Tim just may stick. Takes a lot of balls to be small and volunteer to fight in an illegal underground fight club.

"Why do they call you Bones?" Tim asks, popping his neck and stretching his arms as they stand in the middle of the gym floor.

"Because I break them," Bones says before bringing his massive fist through the air, which is the size of Tim's head. One hit from that thing, no wonder bones break.

Tim ducks quickly, and everyone gasps to watch the little one move between Bones' legs. Tim climbs up him like a tree, wraps an arm around Bones' neck, and presses against his jugular until Bones falls to his knees. His eyes roll back, and he passes out. Tim jumps down like a damn spider monkey and if a pen fell in the room, there's no way it couldn't be heard because no one in this room is breathing.

"Holy shit!" Reaper gasps, then slowly a chant forms, and all the bikers are stomping and yelling, "Braveheart."

Tim looks downright tickled and proud of himself. He's blushing and looks shy, but when he fought, he had the confidence of Bones.

"Prospect, you do this, you can have your patch and the nickname."

"Really?" He pushes those damn frames up his nose again, looking dorky as hell. I've been wondering what he can bring to the club, and he's just proven himself.

"Really, this works out because no one has seen your face, so when you enter the house, they won't be suspicious. It's time for us to plan, fellas," Reaper announces. Boomer comes into the auditorium with a red cheek, giving Sarah a piggyback ride like they used to do when they were younger. Well, I'm glad they patched things over.

It's time to figure this shit out because by tonight I'm going to have my girl in my arms and my mom home where she belongs.

My screwdriver is going to be lodged in the sheriff's forehead, and if there's one thing I know I'm good at, it's how to kill a parent.

20
JULIETTE

Loud music pounds outside, and the walls bend and vibrate with every beat of the bass, but it isn't as loud as the crowd. The roar of cheers from people gathering for the fight or for what comes after it ends. I'm scared out of my mind, confused, and angry. My dad spent so many years training me to fight, but then he ends up doing this? Was it all a ruse just to keep me off his real intentions?

"I'm sorry," Whitney says for the hundredth time. "I know how confusing it must be."

"It just doesn't make sense," I mumble a reply, staring at the wall in front of me. I've traced the same crack in the wall with my eyes for hours.

"Psychopaths rarely do."

Yeah, I'm gathering that.

The familiar clunky metal door slides open at the end of the hall, and laughter follows. I know that laugh anywhere. It's my dad. His heavy footsteps sound my fate as he gets closer. He stands in front of the cell with a beer in his hand, and at some point during the day he changed out of his uniform into black jeans and a black t-shirt.

His hands grip the bars and yanks the door open, sliding it to the left. "Party is about to start, pumpkin." He pops the p with a sly grin, a look of humor on his face. "Come meet your guests. They're really looking forward to it." He comes to the side of the bed, and his hand is cold from the beer he is holding. He pulls my head back and tilts the bottle over my face until the cold carbonation hits my lips and forces its way down throat. Then he moves the neck of the bottle, letting the beer rush over my eyes and face. I sputter, spitting the beer out of my mouth. I wish I had control of my hands because my eyes are burning from the alcohol. "You need to relax. Take another swallow."

"Leave her alone!" Whitney shouts, fighting against the restraints on her wrists to try to stop him.

"Don't make me sew your mouth just, bitch." He spins around and backhands her, his palm connecting to her cheek so hard Whitney's head flies back and smacks against the wall, knocking her out cold.

"Whitney!" I call out as my dad picks me up by my neck and shoves me off the bed.

"Shut up. Get to walking!" His hand lands flat against my back and pushes me forward until my chest hits the metal bars. I cry out when my collarbone hits the bars at an odd angle. My knees buckle, but dear old Dad is there to save me. "Stop being such a fucking klutz." His hold on my arm is so tight, I'm afraid my bone will break. "We don't have all night." He shoves me out the door, and I hit the cell across from mine.

"Oh my god," I whisper when I see two teenage girls handcuffed to their cots, naked, and by the looks of it, drugged out of their mind. "What are you doing to them? Let them go!"

Dad slides the door to my cell shut, keeping a tight hand on my wrist to control me. "Who, them? Don't worry; their cunts are legal." He brushes my hair back from my ear and chuckles. "I had a taste of them this morning. I'm surprised you didn't hear me. They fucking loved it."

"You're a monster," I whisper, staring at two young girls who can't be older than eighteen with bruises on their thighs and needle marks in their arms.

"I'm a businessman, pumpkin. Rent has to get paid." He pushes me forward again, my feet tangling against each other from the inability of gaining control of my momentum forced by my father's hand. "Let's get going."

"Don't do this. I know I have to mean something to you. For you to teach me how to defend myself—"

"You think I taught you that out of love?" He spins me around and slams my back against the wall before entering the door that leads to the loud music and cheering crowd. "Men love a woman who fights them. It makes the encounter that much more … intriguing." He brushes my hair out of my face and pushes it over my shoulder. "Men love the thrill of subduing their victim—oops—I mean woman. Nothing is more thrilling than to see a woman get weaker the more they fight, but we men get stronger when we realize we're winning."

"You won't get away with this," I say with as much venom as I can muster with every ounce of hate I have in my soul for my father. As much love as I used to feel for him, that's how much I despise him right now. If hate were enough, it would kill him where he stands.

"Oh, I've been getting away with it, pumpkin. For years." He bends down to get closer to my face, and I turn my head, jerking away from him. My left cheek presses against rusty metal bars, and my dad kisses the exposed cheek. The man is sickening. "Come on, Juliette. It isn't very nice to keep all these people waiting." He grips my neck and guides me through the door, his fingers pressing against my jugular just enough to make breathing uncomfortable.

I'm not sure what to expect when I walk out the door. A living room? A kitchen? Something that looks like a house, but no, that's not the case at all. All of the walls have been knocked out, and all that I can see is the frame of the house.

Normal house on the outside, empty shell on the inside.

A chain fence blocks wooden bleachers around the walls. People are grasping the fence, shaking the metal, screaming in my face as my father takes me to the middle of the room. It smells of smoke, alcohol, sweat, and blood. I wince when the light turns on, and I look down at my feet, seeing bloodstains on the plywood.

And is that…

A tooth?

That's a tooth. Oh god, what the hell is this place?

"Thank you all for coming out tonight," my dad announces, keeping a tight hold on my wrists. "We have a great show for you. Please, place your bets with Zig. There will be seven rounds. The winner will get my daughter, all to himself, to do with whatever he wants." Deep roars sound from the left, and that's when I see a line of very large men, all shirtless, staring at me with so much want it looks life-threatening.

It probably is.

"We have plenty of women for anyone who needs to take the edge off. Just come see me and pay a flat fee. All but the winner of tonight's fights has to pay. If you're new here, welcome to The Pit. If you're a regular, welcome back. You know the drill." Everyone screams after my dad gets done talking, and the music starts to blare again, shaking the wood under my feet.

"You're going to be saved for the winner, pumpkin. I can't have you all used up. That wouldn't be very good of me," he whispers into my ear, smiling as he waves at the crowd. It's like he's their god or something. "But let's give the fighters something to fight for."

I'm not following until he rips my shirt off my body and tosses it to the section where the fighters are. The men beat on the fence trying to get free as they're teased with my body that I don't want them to have. "This is what you'll win, fellas. Young, beautiful, and I can guarantee her cunt is tight. All for you. You'll get her for one night only."

"No!" I try to wiggle free from my dad's grasp when I realize his plans for me. I'm a trophy, and I doubt this is the last night. It's going to be every night. "I don't want this." I fall down from my efforts of getting loose from his evil fingers. I'm on my knees, and that only makes the fighters froth at the mouth. The entire fence bends and shakes, and for a second I think they're about to break it down. I kick my legs out, and it swipes my dad's legs from underneath him, just like he taught me.

He only falls to his knees, and he grips me by the back of my head and slams my face against the rough plywood of the floor. My entire body falls limp, and I moan in pain when stars burst across my eyes. My surroundings blur.

"She's a fighter too, boys. I made sure of that," he says. "Let the fights begin!" he yells to get the crowd riled up, and everyone screams, waiting for the show to begin.

The clock is ticking, and I don't think Logan will find me before I'm a fighter's prize.

"Come up, pumpkin. Let's get you presentable. Wouldn't want you to look unappealing." He lifts me up by my hair, but I don't have the strength to get up, so he drags me by my brown locks. I lift my hands up to grab my scalp in hopes of alleviating the pressure and sting of my hair follicles.

"Help me," I try to scream, but the pain in my head is stopping me, and the words come out a jumbled, slurred mess. "Someone,"

224

I plead as he drags me down the steps. My tailbone smacks against the wood every time my body drops.

"Shut up. No one worthy comes to this place. You're fucked, pumpkin. And you're going to make me so much money." He opens a door to a bedroom where an older woman is sitting at a vanity, long brown hair cascading down her back while powdering her face. "Make her look good."

"I know." She rolls her eyes and rubs her lips together after applying red lipstick. "This isn't my first rodeo."

"I know. You're going to be the best whore around," my dad purrs and tosses me on the bed. He leaves me there to go push his hands down the front of the woman's lingerie set. "I want some of this later."

"And you'll get it." Her voice sounds familiar, friendly, and comforting.

"Mmm, those tits." He grunts as squeezes her breasts. "I'm going to fuck them then fuck you. You better be ready."

"As ever," the woman tells him in a flirtatious tone, ending on an innocent giggle.

Innocent. Right.

"Make her beautiful," my dad orders and then exits the room, slamming and locking the door behind him.

"Juliette? Juliette!" the woman hisses. "Girly? Are you okay?"

I open my eyes, squinting them when I see Trixie staring at me with concern. She has on a wig and one of the lingerie sets from the store. When everything snaps in place, I roll off the bed to get away from her. "You were in on this! You traitor! I can't believe you would do this to me!" I back myself in a corner, my wrists twinging when my skin gets caught in the metal hinges of the cuffs. I begin to sob, my heart breaking from all the betrayal I'm feeling. I can't believe my friend, the person I've worked with for two years, and my father would do this to me.

"No, girly! Oh, god, no! I swear it, listen to me. I'm only here because Logan came to me and asked for help. He wondered how to safely get in the house without hurting you and the guy he has fighting right now. He didn't want to risk your safety, and I knew a guy, who knew a guy, who knew a guy who wanted to go out with me, and I said I'd go out with him if he got me in here. It's a little confusing, but Trixie has tricks up her sleeve, girly. I'm not going to do anything to you. You're my girly! We are going to get you out of here." She slaps my shoulder, a bit put off that I'd accuse her of turning against me. Can she blame me? Considering …

"Really? And Logan? You let my dad grab you. Why?"

"Because a whore has to play her part. There's a lot you don't know about me, Juliette. Let's keep it that way."

"What's the plan?" I ask as Trixie digs into her hair, pulls out a bobby pin, and easily digs the tiny end into the cuff lock. I give her a questioning look, and she gives me a nervous smile.

"Don't ask," she says and then unlocks the cuffs on my wrist. "As of right now, they're going to go about it the club way. The man who wins gets you, and the Ruthless Kings plan on winning."

"No, they can't! Dad will know—"

"No, your dad doesn't know the prospect, Tim. Cute little guy, might get crushed, but they say that he won't. After he wins, he will come to you, and that's when they're going to storm the place. They have all the chapters with them, girly. This place is about to get burned to the ground."

Yeah, I just hope we aren't in it when it turns to ash.

"I should be in there," I say, pissed off and on edge as I watch the house through the window of the truck Reaper's driving.

"No, you shouldn't be." Badge types away on the computer from the back seat. "You'd think with your emotions and get yourself killed."

"No, I wouldn't. I'm going." I grab the door handle to get out when Reaper grabs my arm to stop me.

"And say you get caught. There's one of you and who knows how many people in there. Let the plan play out; it's a good plan."

"Let Tim win, get Juliette to safety—"

"And my mom? No, there has to be another way. I can't wait that long, Reaper."

"You might not have to," Badge says, turning his laptop around to show me. "It took some digging, but there looks like there's an underground tunnel leading from the sewer. It takes you to the basement. It looks like the tunnel hasn't been used in over a hundred years, so it might not even lead to the house anymore anyway."

"I don't care. I'm going. Where's the entrance to the sewer?" A knock at the window interrupts the plan, on top of the other plan, which doesn't seem like a good idea in the long run, but I have to get in that house.

"Boomer," I say his name through clenched teeth. He always finds the most inopportune moments to interrupt. And, of course, Caster is next to him.

I swear to god, why won't this guy just go away?

I roll down the window, impatient and annoyed. "What?"

"Oh, touchy," Boomer says, smiling at me with his annoying, know-it-all smile.

"Caster," I grumble a greeting.

He smiles too.

Why is everyone smiling? I hate it.

"It's just down the street," Badge says.

"I want to come," Boomer bounces on his feet with excitement, and Caster chuckles.

"Eager. Even with the enemy in ya head, ya positive, Boomer," Caster says.

"My enemy is my friend now; that's why. Kill them. Kill them. Kill them," he chants, replacing the word himself with them. "I'm taking Reaper's advice. And I have a feeling we have some killing to do?"

I double check to make sure I have my tool, touching the side of my head. I open the door and take one last look at the house. If she isn't in there, I don't know what I'll do. It's my last hope of finding Juliette. I run to the right, away from the house, and Boomer's boots are right behind me. I follow the blacktop of the road into the night, staring at the streetlights that line the street.

When I get to the intersection, a rundown white house is on the right with a few people standing on the porch, but they stay away from us. Good, they must have gotten the message from their friend. I come to a stop and look around for the sewer entrance. As I suspect, it's in the middle of the road. I run over to the round metal manhole and squat down, grabbing ahold of the top. "Damn this is heavy," I grunt, using every ounce of strength I have to push it aside. Metal grinds against the pavement, and it's loud, causing my ears to ring.

"Alright. Apparently, there's an old tunnel that leads to the basement of the house. It might not be in use but—"

"But nothing. We'll blow whatever shit that's in our way, out of the way. You know I come prepared. Let's go save your girl." Boomer slaps my shoulder with positivity that I've never seen from him before.

"I'm coming too—"

"You keep your witchy shit to yourself, okay? Those are the rules," I tell Caster as I descend the ladder into darkness. I jump down and land in shallow water, my boots splashing up filth along my jeans. It smells like death, and the snicker of little rodents tell

231

me we're surrounded by rats. Boomer jumps down next, then Caster.

"This tunnel has—"

"Shut up, Caster. I'm so close to ramming this screwdriver in your skull," I stop him from saying anything else about the tunnel. It's probably haunted by bad shit or whatever, and I don't want to know the details.

"Ya need to be open to the possibility that there are other things out there besides normal."

"If you think what we're doing is normal, you're out of your fucking mind. The little witchy nonsense has fried your brain." I wind my finger by my head, a way of calling him crazy, and follow the sewer in the only direction that it goes. It's dark, creepy, and the only sound bouncing off the curved walls are the little nails of rats and our boots sloshing through the mess that's in the water.

My hands are twitching for violence, to spew my hatred into the bastard who calls himself a father to Juliette.

"You love this woman despite the fear you feel of one day being a father that your children hate," Caster says.

I let out one long breath and push Caster against the slick dirty wall, my arm on his chest and the screwdriver teasing his temple. "You listen to me—don't talk to me like you know me. Don't speak to me. You don't know shit about me or how I feel. And whatever vibes you get, don't feel like you have to share them." I shove off him, and he nods but does so with a smile.

Fucking can't wait for the New Orleans chapter to get out of here.

"Boomer, can you not play catch with the grenade? It's making me a little nervous, but it's good to know not a lot of things change." I watch as the grenade flies up in the air, then back in his palm, up, down, up, down, until he finally puts it in his cut pocket.

"You suck the fun out of everything," Boomer pouts, kicking the water and flinging it against the wall, scaring a few rats away.

We come to a part of the sewer that has four metal bars separating us, and at the end there seems to be a door of some kind. "This is it, but how are we going to get through?" The rust digs into my skin as I grip and pull. I make a mental note to get a tetanus shot. The bars bend, but they don't break. "Fuck!" my curse echoes down the sewer line. "That has to be it."

"Let me blow it up."

"We don't know what will happen to the rest of the sewer, Boomer. You have anything less lethal in your pockets?" He pulls out a miniature stick of dynamite. I remember those from fighting with the Jersey chapter.

"They make a punch, but it isn't nearly as fun. Step back." Boomer sounds less than thrilled to have to be doing this. He lifts a packet of matches to light the fuse, but I grab his wrist at the last moment before he blows us to hell. "What are you doing?" he asks, pouting his bottom lip like a toddler.

"You're going to kill us if you light that. There could be gases in the air or something," I warn, tightening my fingers around his wrist.

Instead of realization or panic, something else flickers in his eyes. He wants to see if there are gases in the sewer so he can blow this bitch up. Crazy bomb-wielding motherfucker.

"Fine," he resigns, but I can see the wheels turning in his head as he thinks about burning the sewer to the ground. "What would you have me do? I didn't come with anything else. My pockets are full of grenades and dynamite." His voice bounces off the sewer walls, echoing down the tunnel along with the tiny scratches of rats.

There has to be something. I feel around the top of the archway where the bars meet the cement. Only to feel that they are welded to metal, and the metal is drilled into the cement. I can't hide the cocky smirk when something as simple as my screwdriver will remedy this. "Watch and learn, fellas." I pluck my tool—my weapon, my everything—and insert the simple flathead into the old rusted screws. "Fucking hell, this might not work," I grunt as I twist the screwdriver, putting as much strength as I can into the rusted metal.

"Come on, mon ami. You can do it. Think of Juliette," Caster tries to encourage me, and an image of her crying for me, bruised, and god knows what else has me grabbing onto strength I didn't realize existed inside me. The cement and ancient metal grind together, a new sound I despise, like nails on a chalkboard, until the bolt clanks onto the floor, landing in a filth-infested puddle.

"Not as cool as dynamite, but whatever. It works." Boomer kicks the screw on the ground, pouting.

I'm sweating by the time I get the third screw out and decide it's lose enough to try to kick in now. I wipe my eyes to get the salty liquid from blinding me and lift my foot, hitting the semi-loose bars. The bars groan but don't give.

"Fuck, come on," I say in desperation, and Caster places his hand on my chest, stopping me from trying again.

"Let me, mon ami. Save your strength. Boomer, on the count of three. Come on." Caster jerks Boomer to hide behind him. "One, two—"

"Wait. On three or after three."

"Zut, Boomer! Three. On Three." It's the first time I've ever heard Caster annoyed, and hearing him curse is hilarious.

"It matters. Just saying." Boomer lifts his hands, pleading his case.

"One, two, three—" Caster and Boomer slam their steal-toe boots against the bars, and the metal snaps in half, some rusted bits crumbling to the ground.

Boomer makes an explosion sound with his mouth, making it seem as if we did blow the door down. "So anti-climactic." He sighs with a breath of disappointment.

No doubt that made a lot of racket. We need to hurry. I grab the bars and step through, hissing when one of the sharp, jagged ends scratches my arm and brings blood to the surface.

"Okay, one of you needs to stay down here. I don't know how many girls there are or if it's just Juliette and my mom. But I can't help them out. They have to meet you down here."

"I'll stay," Caster says.

"Good. Let's go, Boomer." I lift my leg and step over the old, broken bars that have been there a lot longer than I've been on this earth. We gently step through the debris to make sure there isn't any lingering boom left in the dynamite, and then run to the door. "It's been used. Look." I point at the scratches on the cement from the door swinging open and closed.

"Look." Boomer points to the empty space next to the tunnel, a part that isn't blocked off, and it's filled with bones and decomposing bodies. "Oh my god," he whispers, staring at the scene in front of us. "They're all women."

"They use them and when they're done with them, they bring them—" I can't finish the sentence. I lift my boot and slam the door in, only to be welcomed by a guard. I shove my screwdriver between his eyes without hesitation.

"Damn, you're quick with that," Boomer says.

"There's no time not to be." My weapon drips with fresh blood, and it brings that necessary fuel I need to kill again. The hallway itself is empty, but another door comes to view. I kick that one in, feeling my knee pulse with pain from the amount of strength it takes to break it down. There are two guards here, and Boomer takes one, then I take the other, thrusting the tool in his stomach, then his head.

"Only a few seconds," Boomer says with a crazy grin, licking his lips as the guy's eyes widen while Boomer has his hands over the guard's mouth. Boomer pushes the guard into the hallway we just came out of, and the guy's stomach bursts, sending a gory bout of blood over the walls.

"Gross."

"Awesome," Boomer beams.

"Help us," a small voice comes from the inside, and Boomer and I follow the crying plea. When I step foot inside the basement, there are six cells lining each side of the wall and pleasurable moans coming from the other end.

With slow, stealthy steps, I make my way toward the nightmare unfolding. I find the door open and a man pulling up his pants after fucking a girl who looks too drugged out. Her body is limp, and he didn't even use a fucking condom. He took what she didn't want to give.

"What the fuck do you think you're doing?" I charge at him and get a firm grip of his shirt collar, and that's when I notice the ankles of the girls chained spread eagle. Sick fucking bastard.

"Wait your turn! I paid!" He nearly falls over from his jeans being wrapped around his ankles, and his small cock bobs.

"You're dead," I whisper in his ear before plunging the tool in his balls and pinning him to the wall. He tries to cry out, but I muffle his screams with my palm. I pull the screwdriver free and then make the guy grab his cock, find the slit where he pisses, and drive the screwdriver inside, hoping it's tearing him apart. "Sick fucks like you don't deserve the privilege of life." I rip the metal out and keep plunging it through his entire body, landing the final blow to his heart.

"Boomer? Get her out of those cuffs, and let her have your shirt or something." I wipe the blood on my jeans, and when Boomer sees the girl on the cot, a shaky breath falls from his lips.

"Reminds me of Scarlett in a way. If I hadn't have gotten to her... This could have been her life. A prostitution ring." Boomer clears his throat and makes his way to the girl, covering her with his leather cut. "You're going to be okay."

"Don't. No," the girl slurs. "No."

"You're okay," Boomer says again.

"She doesn't know what's going on. Just get her out of there," I say and then make my way toward the next cell. It takes some doing to open the lock to the old dungeon cell, but I manage. All the girls are drugged, but they can stand. One girl is dead, overdose it looks like, and I know she'll have to come too. Her parents deserve to bury her.

"Follow the hallway. You'll meet a man there, Caster. He's going to take you for help, okay?" I tell the group of five. They're all trembling, crying, filthy dirty, but they don't ask questions; they hightail it out of there. With a deep breath, I make my way to the last cell, and Boomer is carrying the other girl out of hers.

"I'm taking her to Caster. She's too fucked up to walk. I'll be back."

I nod and open the last cell, not bothering to look inside because I know what I'm going to find. When I slide the door open, one cot is empty, but the other has an unconscious woman on it. She's clothed, and my heart pounds in my chest when I recognize

238

the cut she's wearing. "Mom?" I run over to her side and move her hair out of the way and hang my head with relief. She's alive. Thank fuck, she's alive. "Mom, wake up. Come on. I need you to wake up." I shake her shoulders, and she groans, slowly shaking her head. "Mom, come on."

Her eyes flutter open, and I work on unlocking the cuffs from her wrists and ankles. "Logan? Is that you?" She stares at me with disbelief and confused, glazed eyes. "Am I dreaming?"

"No, I'm here." I cup her face and smile, holding back the tears. "I'm so fucking glad you're okay. I'm going to get you out of here."

"Juliette. He took her." She holds her head when I help her sit up. "In the house."

"Okay, I'm going to need you to follow that hallway to my friend Caster, okay? I'll get Juliette."

"You came. My baby boy." Her eyes fall to my bloody jeans, seeing the red liquid on the screwdriver. "You have to do what you have to."

"Can you walk?"

She nods and sways when she stands. My hands fall to her shoulder to help steady her. "I'm fine. Go. Who knows what that man has planned and, Logan?" My mom grabs my arm and frowns. "The sheriff, you wouldn't remember him. It's been too long, but he's your dad's stepbrother and the prospect who helped take care of your dad's body? Brass kicked him out of the club a few years back and told the sheriff everything. And you and Juliette..." She cups my face, and her eyes water with a sad smile. "You know each other. You met once while—"

"The little girl I watched while—" I remember the day. My dad and his stepbrother took turns on my mom, and I had to drown out her screams by turning up the television. "That was Juliette?"

"Bring her home, Logan." My mom pats my cheek and walks out of the cell. Her Property of Brass cut stares at me before she hangs left and disappears down the hall.

Now it's just me and Juliette's father. I'll fight to the death. I flip the screwdriver in my hand and march down the cement corridor. Opening the door, I kill the first man I see.

Ziggy.

"Looks like you didn't zag, Zig," I tell him, his skull crunching under my boot as I yank my weapon from his head. The crowd is roaring, banging their feet on the floor as the fight rumbles on. The hall is dark, and I'm not worried about anyone seeing me right now. Tim is on a guy's shoulders, sweating, looking beat to death with half of his face swollen. He wraps his legs around the guy's neck, then twists, and the giant falls to the floor, shaking the entire foundation of the house. Tim flips off the guy before he can get trapped under deadweight.

Braveheart is impressive. I'll give him that much.

"Looks like we have a winner, folks," the sheriff holds up Tim's hands, his bony chest rising and falling with heavy pants as he tries to catch his breath. "You aren't going to be disappointed."

I step forward into the light for the sheriff to see me, and Tim takes that as the cue to run toward the other end of the house where he must know where Juliette is.

"Too late. The winner is already going to claim his prize," the sheriff singsongs.

I don't correct him. And while the sheriff and I have a stare down, Reaper, Voodoo, Bones, Bullseye, and thirty other members bust through the door. "Cops will be here in five minutes," Badge announces, and all the members pull out a gun from their cut, aiming at the crowd, daring for someone to try to leave.

"I have five minutes to kill you," I taunt the sheriff.

"I'll only need one to finally put you where you belong. Six-feet under, just like your dad."

I lift my fist, because I want to relish in taking the man's life, and slam it across his face. "I'm nothing like him."

"Logan!" Juliette's voice is music to my ears and the distraction I don't need. The sheriff takes the time to tackle me to the ground. "Logan!" I hear her cry for me, and it surges power in my muscles, in my veins, and for the first time in my life, I use love for fuel instead of hate.

And it gives me more strength than rage ever did.

I watch in horror as Logan gets tackled to the ground. Derek lifts his fist and throws the heavy punches into Logan's face. Even from here, I can hear the flesh against flesh and see the mental rage in Derek's eyes as he beats Logan. He's no longer my father, the man who raised me. He's the enemy. A vile, disgusting being who doesn't deserve his next breath.

The crowd is quiet as a large man wearing a Ruthless MC cut aims the barrel of his gun at a man in the front row, then points at the man in the second row. People notice they are no longer reaping the benefits of the horrid event and are about to fall victim for supporting such a vile act.

Logan kicks Derek and goes to plunge the screwdriver in the enemy's head when the psycho who raised me knocks it out of Logan's hands.

"We need to get you out of here, come on." Tim tries to push me through the back door, but I plant my feet. Trixie is tugging on my arms, giving me a pleading look to listen to Tim.

"I'm not leaving Logan. Why aren't they helping him? What kind of brothers are you?" I push Tim's sweaty chest.

"It's personal with Logan. He told us not to interfere."

"I'm not leaving without him, and that's final," I snarl, pushing Tim away from me along with Trixie. I run to the ring, and Derek grins at me when he kicks Logan's side. "Logan!"

"Aw, what is it, pumpkin? Does this bother you?" He kicks Logan again, flipping him onto his back.

I cup my hands over my mouth and watch as Logan struggles to get to his hands and knees, only for Derek to slam his boot into Logan's ribs again. Logan's hand reaches for his screwdriver, and Derek doesn't notice since his eyes are locked on me. Logan moves quicker than I thought he could and rams the weapon in the sheriff's thigh, causing him to cry out and fall to the floor, clutching his leg.

"How does that feel? Soon you'll meet the same death as your fucked-up stepbrother, and I can't fucking wait to be the one to do it." Logan stands on his strong legs, his wide chest heaving as he stares down at the sheriff. He bends his knee and kicks with so much force, Derek's head slams back, and blood gushes down his face.

And still the man laughs. "Is that all you got?" Derek rams an elbow in Logan's side, and the screwdriver tumbles to the ground, rolling away to the end of the ring where the fence meets the plywood.

As Logan fights with the crook, I drop to my hands and knees and crawl toward the screwdriver. My eyes lift to check my surroundings, and Reaper looks from me to Logan with saucer-wide eyes. He takes a step forward to get me out of there, but I shake my head, telling him to stay where he is. He doesn't look happy. He looks fucking pissed. It will be worth it soon. The closer I get to the screwdriver, the faster I crawl.

Blood drips from it in thick strings. My stomach rolls when I think about having to wrap my hand around the slick blood on the handle, but I have to. I turn my head and see Derek staggering. Both him and Logan are exhausted, circling each other to prepare for the final strike.

I snatch the screwdriver within my grasp, and sirens wail in the distance causing panic. Logan takes advantage of Derek's distraction and punches him again. Logan has his back turned toward me as I get to my feet, and his shirt is wet with sweat from the humidity and exertion. Derek's eyes land on mine, and he smiles, teeth bloodied and broken. The man who threw me all the birthday parties, held me while I cried, told me bedtime stories, made dinner, and went shopping with me, looks at me with so much hate, and all the memories I have turn to dust. He betrayed me.

He betrayed other women. Women he was supposed to keep safe and protect. He's the sheriff; it's his job.

And he failed, miserably.

I charge at him with all the fucking hate I can muster. My heart feels like it's been taken over by something evil, something dark, and whatever it is numbs my brain. All I can think about is killing him myself. I hate him. I hate him so fucking much.

"You don't have it in you!" he shouts, spitting a wad of blood on the floor.

Logan turns around on a quick spin, and he tries to stop me, but he reaches for me too late. My piece of shit father realizes that I do have it in me, and he tries to plead for his life, but there's no stopping it.

I sink the sharp screwdriver between his eyes until the damn tool comes out on the other side of his head, getting locked in the fence. He moves his mouth to speak, and his eyes look up to mine. I bend down, giving him the same twisted grin he gave me when he locked me in the cell. "It looks like I do have it in me, Dad," I sneer the name, the endearment he took for granted, and watch his pupils go wide as the last of his breath leaves his lungs.

Logan spins me around and hauls me to his chest, his hand burying in my hair. He picks me up, and I wrap my legs around his waist. "You're real. You're here," my voice stutters and breaks as my body quakes from the adrenaline.

"Of course, I'm here. I love you," he tells me. "I love you so much. I'll do anything for you, little sparrow, even if it means setting you free from a cage."

"I love you too." I know I'm about to break, about to cry about what I had to do, but Logan pulls away and cups my face.

His face is a mess with sweat, dirt, and blood. "I never wanted you to have to do that. I wanted to do it for you. I wanted to kill him. I never wanted you to feel that."

"Feel what?"

"All that hate," he says. "It's poison."

I lay my hand over his heart, the one carved into his chest and nod. "But the cure to that is you, Logan. It's love. Your love."

He smashes his lips against mine as the police enter the door. Logan breaks the kiss and snatches the screwdriver out of the sheriff's head and tucks it in his pocket.

"This is what happened," Badge starts to explain to the cops, and Logan leans his forehead against mine.

"Let's get you home," he says.

I lay my head on his shoulder and then gasp, sitting up when I remember Tyrant. "Oh god, Tyrant! He died. He tried to—"

"I got him in time, Juliette. He's okay."

I hold back tears of relief because I know if I break, I won't stop crying for hours. I can't believe I just killed a man. One by one, the police arrest the people in the crowd, taking the scum away that supports things like this. It's disgusting. It's hard to believe that people will do something so despicable for money.

"Where are they going?" I ask an hour later as all the cops leave.

"Badge asked for a favor. We're going to take care of the house. The women are safe and on their way to the hospital, along with my mom."

"She was nice," I tell him. "I hate I had to meet her that way."

"Me too." He places a soft kiss on my forehead, and nothing has ever felt better.

"I didn't get to cut out his tongue," Tongue pouts.

"So go," Reaper says to him.

"He's dead. Where's the fun in that?" Tongue marches away in an angry tantrum, and the guy who calls himself Boomer runs out of the house.

"Oh shit," Logan picks me up and swings me into his arms, and everyone moves across the street, behind the bikes.

"What?"

"You'll see."

"Everyone, get back!" Boomer shouts. As he runs, the first few explosions rock the ground. Flames engulf the house of nightmares along with black smoke. "Wait, that's not all!" He rubs his hands together and counts, "Five, four, three, two," and he points to the house right as fireworks jet through the air, whistling and popping as they make their way toward the starry sky and explode into beautiful crackles of different colors. Boomer jumps up and down and looks at us for confirmation. "It's good, right? I've been playing around with a few things, and boom. It's pretty great!" He watches the fireworks go off one by one with fascination.

I don't have it in me to be happy when I know I killed my dad, and his body is inside burning in the heat of hell.

"You okay?" Logan asks, moving my hair off my shoulder.

"I don't know."

"Let's go home and get some rest. We aren't needed here anymore." Logan picks me up in his arms and carries me to the truck. Exhaustion finally hits, and I lean my head against his shoulder, closing my eyes just for a second.

One quick little second.

I'm jostled awake when Logan carries me through the clubhouse door. "We're here," he says, kicking the door shut with his foot. Only a few guys are here, and I don't recognize them, but since Logan isn't worried about the men, I'm not either. He opens up the door to his room, and Yeti is curled up in his dog bed, snoring and not even waking up when we close the bedroom door. "Tyrant has to stay at the vet for a few days, but he'll be back soon. Maybe when you're up for it, you'll move in here with me. I'll build you your dream home on the property, away from the party of the clubhouse."

I'm not sure if I'm dreaming this or not. It sounds like I am. I'm so drowsy, and I can't decide what's real and what's a dream.

"That sounds perfect." Whether it's a dream or not, I have to say yes.

"Yeah?" He pushes my hair out of my face and smiles.

"Yeah, Logan." I lean into his touch and sigh, feeling relieved. I shouldn't feel that way, but the world is a better place without my father in it.

"I know what you did is hard to wrap your head around, and if you ever want to talk about it, I can relate. It took a long time for me to realize that real love is so much stronger than hate. I didn't think it was possible, but then I met you, and you shook me up, little sparrow. You shined a much-needed light on the darkest part of my soul." He leans in and gives me a slow, languid kiss. It isn't the kind of kiss that gets the body roaring to a lust-burning level. It's the kind that soothes havoc, that slows the wild heart and the hurting mind. It's the kind that reminds me that reality can be so much better than fantasy.

It's the kind of kiss that I never want to end.

Logan is slowly possessing me, but he isn't the demon—he's the archangel, and he has rescued me from the devil. He thinks he's my damnation, but Logan is my salvation, and I know I'll be protected at all costs. He's right and wrong. A mixture of a saint and a sinner. The man who realizes that sometimes you have to do something bad for the greater good. He's the calm and the storm. The rage and hate. The love and the passion. He's a killer and a lover.

He's the kind of man a woman should never invite between her legs, but once she does, she's addicted, regardless of the blood he's bathed his hands with.

He's made me realize there's a difference between a demon and the devil. A demon slowly takes over your body until you don't know who you are anymore. The devil takes and steals and doesn't care who he hurts in the process as long as he achieves his goal.

Logan is both.

He'll do anything to have me, even though he's already

possessed me. The silky strands of love with the barbed thorns of bad intentions create Logan.

I'll take that kind of man over any other kind.

He's everything.

I wake to the sound of Juliette screaming and begging for her life. I reach toward the lamp and turn it on, and my eyes wince on instinct from the quick burst of light. I don't care about the small inconvenience, not when I see her breaking out in a hot sweat, her skin slick and shiny, and her eyes pinched. She tosses and turns, clutching the sheet to her chest as she tries to fight off the attacker in her dreams.

"Juliette!" I raise my voice in hopes to penetrate her dreams. I grab her by the arms and shake her.

"Logan!" she sobs, still not waking up, and my heart clenches that she can't hear me.

"I'm here, little sparrow." I bring my lips to her ear and whisper, "I'm here. You're safe. I love you. You're safe. Wake up."

Yeti cries when she doesn't listen to me. I feel his pain. I hate this. She's crying out for me to save her, but I'm here. I'm right fucking here.

"Juliette," I yell her name and shake her again, this time picking up her body before slamming it down on the bed. I'm careful not to hurt her, but she has to wake up.

Her eyes finally snap open, and they're glossed over from the nightmare. Sweat beads above her top lip, and her chest is rising in hard, frantic rhythms.

"Logan," she gasps my name, and I run my knuckles down her cheek, smiling in relief.

"Hey, you're safe. You're here with me," I place her hand on my chest to feel my heart, and she breaks down, the entire event finally slamming against her. I hold her as she clutches me for dear life, as if I'll vanish into thin air.

She buries her face in my shoulder, and her tears wet my sore skin from the fight I had with her father. I have a few cracked ribs and a swollen cheek, but it's a small price to pay to have her in my arms again.

Her lips press against my shoulder, and I stroke her hair with my hand, crooning that everything is going to be okay. Our past is officially laid to rest and now all we have to do is build our future. Her mouth moves up my neck, pressing wet, desperate kisses along my jugular. She pants in my ear, and the needy sounds drive me over the edge. I want her more than anything, but I'm not sure she's all there mentally right now.

"Juliette, you're shaken up," I say as she kisses down my

chest, paying extra attention to the purple bruises along my ribs.

"I need to feel you, Logan. I need you, please." She drops to her stomach and yanks the sheet from my waist to reveal my erection curving up my belly. "Don't deny me," she says. "I need this. I want to erase—"

I put my finger to her lips. "Take what you need from me, little sparrow. I'm always here for you."

She doesn't hesitate. She wraps her lips around my cock, and her tongue flicks the piercing through my crown, and my back bends off the bed. No woman I've never been has played with my piercings. They usually ignore them and pretend they aren't there because they're intimidated.

Not my Juliette.

She strokes her tongue over the Jacob's ladder, and the rods rub deliciously against my shaft. I tangle my hand in her hair as she peeks those beautiful green eyes at me, watching me, watching her lips stretch to accommodate me.

I notice that we like to watch each other, and it gives me an idea to put a mirror on the ceiling in the house we'll have together one day.

Juliette tries to take me to the root, but she gags, clenching her throat muscles around my cock. I moan, thrusting my hips off the bed from how fucking good it feels. "You better stop, little sparrow. I'm going to fill that mouth."

She shakes her head but keeps sucking me.

"No? I can't hold back. You better get off." I try to warn her, but she grins around the mouthful of cock. "Juliette!" I shout her name, and it comes out more as a whine because I need to fucking come now. My balls are aching, and right when I'm about to fill that wicked mouth, she pops off me and straddles me, thrusting herself down on my sensitive cock with one stroke.

"Oh, fuuuckk," I groan, throwing my head back as I release my cum inside her willing cunt. "Fuck, oh, fuck, yes." My toes curl from how amazing the switch from her mouth to her hot sheath feels.

"That's where I needed you," she whimpers, and the erotic sound has me snapping my eyes open to look at the goddess rutting her hips against me. My hands fall to her waist, following the smooth motions of her body with my arms as she uses me. Her entrance is wet, slick from my cum, and as she grinds against me, I thrust up, so she gets more of me while her clit gets a small tease from my pelvis.

I sit up, wrap one arm around her waist, and take her mouth in a desperate kiss; my attempt to suck the soul from her body to become one with mine. I swallow her greedy whimpers and feed my desire as she rides me.

"You're so beautiful." I run my hands over her heavy tits, before moving to her neck and gripping the back of it. I look down to watch her body swivel. "I can't believe I get to be inside you." I don't mean to say that out loud, but I'm so enamored by the thought of a woman like Juliette, so good, giving her body to me to take care of. And I swear, I'll always take care of her. I flip her onto her back and lift her leg around my waist, driving as deep as I can into her pussy.

"Yes, Logan. Logan, harder."

"I don't want to hurt you."

In a quick move I'm not expecting, she grabs the screwdriver from the nightstand and places it underneath my chin. "I said to fuck me. I'll let you know if you hurt me."

The threat and her feisty nature make another orgasm threaten, but a growl builds from the challenge. I knock the screwdriver out of her hand and carefully grab the part of her arm that isn't bruised, pin it to her chest, and flip her over onto her stomach. Without warning, I drive into her tight cunt, causing her to cry out in pleasure. I keep her head tilted to the side, showing the long elegant curve of her neck, making sure me and everyone else in this house can hear her screams.

"Like this? You like being fucked by my cock, don't you?" I slam against her as hard as I can, moving the bed forward. The headboard bangs against the wall. "Look at you, taking me so good. Fuck, Juliette. This pussy is perfect." I don't know where I find the energy to fuck her like this. Her ass jiggled with every quick thrust, and my sack slaps against her folds, trying to find her clit.

Keeping one hand on her lower back, I reach around and grip the headboard for more leverage so I can shorten my thrusts and speed them up. I watch her pussy suck me in, her pretty pink walls trying to keep me inside every time I pull out. My bicep is straining, and my abs burn along with the severe ache in my ribs as I flex my body to ram into her.

"Logan, oh god, I'm going to come! I'm going to—" Her mouth falls open on a silent scream as a gush of her hot slick drops down my shaft. So warm, and her walls clench and spasm around me, but I'm nowhere near done with her since she pulled an orgasm from me already.

"That's it, little sparrow," I bring my lips down on her neck. "Try to fly away from me; I dare you." I flatten my tongue and lick the sweaty skin to her ear. "I'll just catch you."

"I'll let you catch me," she moans, pressing her face harder against the pillow. "Nowhere else I'd rather be."

I grip her hips and flip her to her back, and her tits bounce since I'm still fucking her without stopping. I bring my other hand to the headboard and hold on tight. The wood cracks the harder I grip to plummet her cunt. I watch her body react to me. Her nipples are red and swollen, and her eyes are closed, and she bites her plump bottom lip. Her cheeks are flushed, and she moans my name over and over again.

"Sing for me," I slam against her, and one of the bed boards under the mattress breaks, sending the box spring to the floor, but she doesn't even notice.

"Logan." She shakes her head.

"I said fucking sing for me." I wrap my hand around her throat and lift her until she's sitting on top of me.

She rolls her hips and lets out a harmonic moan when my

cock head drags along the spot inside her. It's the most beautiful sound, and it causes my eyes to roll back to my head. "You're in my soul, Logan."

I grin, loving how wet her cunt is making it a slick pool for my cock. "If your soul is your pussy, then I'm about ten inches deep, claiming it as mine."

"Yours," she says with parted lips.

"What's that?" I sneer.

"Yours," she screams as her body bows, and she claws at my chest like a fucking cat in heat, and she's depending on me to curve the need.

"And I'm yours, Juliette." I slide my fingers over her jaw, and our eyes meet, our breaths mingling as we pant. Her pace slows, and I wrap my arms around her waist to pull us closer together. Chest to chest, I kiss her heart and pour every ounce of emotion I have for her with every slow intrusion of my cock.

Every wet glide of her pussy brings me closer, and the closer I get to coming, the tighter I hold onto her. I'm afraid she'll disappear again. I dig my nails into her back, clutching her to me like a lifeline thrown at me in raging seas.

My life before her was like drowning in the waves of darkness. I could barely breathe; I suffocated. Juliette is like coming up for that first breath of air, every damn second I'm with her.

Her breathing speeds up, and her hands clutch onto my neck, her body bending back as I hold onto her hips. I eye her neck and tits while the tips of her hair tickle my thighs as she orgasms again, her pussy sucking my cum right from my tight sack.

I bury my face against her chest, right where that beautiful fucking heart is that changed my life, and grunt as I fill her up again, painting her walls with my hot seed. We collapse together, our bodies quaking from the aftershocks of pleasure.

"I think we broke the bed," I state, looking around to notice a crack down the middle of the headboard and the bed slightly tilted to the left.

"That's when you know it's good." She giggles and lays her head on my chest, right where Reaper carved his warning on my skin. "Did this happen because of me?"

I run my hands through her hair and hum. "Yes, but don't blame yourself. I owed him a punishment, and not listening to him about staying away from you pushed him over the edge."

"It's brutal."

"It's the MC life, little sparrow, but it's the life I live."

"As long as I live it with you, I'll be okay." She yawns. Her lips kiss my chest, and she sighs happily and falls back to sleep in a record amount of time.

Juliette has showed me that the most powerful entity in existence is love and that hate no longer has a permanent home here.

Three weeks later

"No, I don't want to go," I tell Trixie who is shoving me on the stage for opening night of Kings Club. "You can't make me!" I stare at the curtain blocking me and the crowd of people waiting to hear music. Logan's live band canceled at the last minute, and now he doesn't have anyone to perform, and the entire place is packed with bikers, Vegas locals, and tourists.

"I can't." I shake my head, feeling the stage fright. My head is spinning, and the nerves are churning. "I've never done this before. I can't, Trixie." Sweat has taken over my entire body, and the more I keep rubbing my hands against my dress, the tackier they become.

Logan has worked so hard to get this place up and running after everything that happened. The other motorcycle chapters stayed behind to help him, and magically it ended up so beautiful with dark red lights and black velvet booths. Then there are lamps dropping from the ceilings to give it a low glow.

"Girly, Logan needs you. He is freaking out because people are leaving, and this night sets precedent for all the other nights."

She had me at 'Logan needs you' and it still doesn't take away the nerves.

"I have your favorite Nora Jones song at the ready. Are you?"

"No, but I'll do it."

"That a girl!" Trixie shoves me out from the long red curtain, and I stumble on stage, my heels clicking against the old wooden planks. The entire club falls silent as everyone stares at me. My eyes search for Logan who is at the bar, talking to Pirate who is drunkenly making drinks. He slaps Logan's chest to get his attention, then points to me on stage.

Logan turns to me, and I see the panic in his eyes. Trixie is right—he needs me, and I can't fail him; especially when he has been there for me. Smoke clings to the air, creating a light veil through the atmosphere.

I walk up to the microphone and the instrumental music of Nora Jones. I let out a shaky breath and stay locked in an intimate gaze with Logan. Knowing he's here is enough to have the first note pouring out. After the first twenty seconds, I relax and hold the classic microphone with a delicate hand, rubbing it up and down sexually, pretending it's Logan to help me put on a show.

I sing to him. I sing for him because if he wasn't here, if this wasn't his club, I wouldn't be here. I bust out the last note and crescendo and then end on a slight whisper. My breath against the mic causes static in the speakers, and I take a step back.

Everyone is still silent.

I swallow, wondering if I sounded that bad, but simultaneously everyone stands, claps, and cheers. Logan runs to me and jumps onto the stage, wearing a Kings Club shirt. It's black, and the name of the club in on the left breast.

"That was the best thing I've ever heard. Damn, I think I just found myself a singer every Friday and Saturday night. What do you say?"

"What? Seriously?" I gape at him, waiting to see if he's joking.

"Seriously. No one else I want here besides you. What do you think?"

"I'll do it for you." I wrap my arms around his neck and smile before he owns my lips in a hot kiss.

Catcalls and whistles sound as the crowd tempts us to kiss harder and longer. "I love you, little sparrow."

"I love you too." Logan waves to the crowd and drags me through the back and behind the curtain. Trixie is jumping up and down, clapping.

"Not right now, Trixie. I'm about to fu—"

"Tool!" Poodle's voice echoes through the backstage, and Bullseye, Reaper, and Sarah follow us back here.

Logan closes his eyes in annoyance. "What, Poodle? What

do you want?"

"Tool, your fucking mutt is dead. You hear me? Dead!" he shouts and then smiles with nothing but love at me. "You have a beautiful voice, Juliette."

"Thanks," I answer him, shifting my weight on my feet.

"You"—he points at Tool. "My Lady is pregnant! Fucking pregnant! Your damn dog fucked her, and now her show figure is done. Forever. You hear me, Tool? I'm going to kill him."

"How do you know it was Yeti?" Logan crosses his arms and stares at Poodle, bulging his biceps.

"Because there isn't another dog in the house that would mount Lady like … like an animal."

"Yeti is nothing but a gentleman!" Tool defends his dog, and I roll my eyes. I can't believe this is an actual conversation.

"Psh!" Poodle snorts. "Like father, like son. If you're banging away every night, it's no wonder where he learns it from!"

"Oh, you sonofa—" Tool launches himself at Poodle, and I decide to walk away toward the bar.

"Me too, girly," Trixie says, sliding her arms through mine.

"Me three," Sarah loops her arm through my other arm.

"Men," I say with a shake of my head as I lean against the long wooden bar. Pirate is making a drink behind the bar. On the wall above the alcohol shelves is the screwdriver Logan used to carry around. Logan decided to retire, wanting to officially put the past behind us, so he keeps a screwdriver on him at all times now; with a yellow handle instead of a blue one.

That one damn screwdriver holds the memory of Logan killing his father and me killing mine.

It's time to focus on the future now, and Tool has been using the screwdriver to help Skirt build our house.

Logan is good at loving me, something I think surprises the badass biker. We killed the hate the moment the screwdriver drove through my father's head.

Hate is a tool, Tool no longer uses.

Only love lives here now.

ACKNOWLEDGMENTS

To my Ruthless Readers, thanks for taking a chance and starting this journey with me.

Jenifer Porter Hughes, thank you for supporting me and so kindly offering notes and suggestions.

Wander, as always, thanks for sharing your talent and taking the perfect images. Still amazes me every day that I have your images on my cover.

Andrey, I'm not sure what I did to deserve you in my corner, but thank you. Your kindness has been such a blessing in my life.

Donna thanks for always being there ready to help or offer advice

Give Me Books and all the blogs that are always sharing and reviewing my books, thank you.

To My Favorite, I love you to the moon and back.

To my instigator, I couldn't ask for anyone better to make bad decisions with.

Silla, as always, thanks for being amazing! You take the role of anybody I need at that point in time, and I know it can't be easy, but I really do appreciate it.

To my other half, thanks for always having my back.

Harloe, as always, thank you for being so awesome.

Mom, thanks for helping me get this off the ground. For keeping calm when all I want to do is panic. For reminding me that even though I'm struggling now, all my hard works is gonna pay off.

Lisa, as always, thanks for your friendship and thanks for always being there.

Austin, thanks for always being so front and center in my life. Y'all are the greatest.

Made in the USA
Monee, IL
29 June 2020